DOCTOR · WHO

The Eyeless

LANCE PARKIN

2 4 6 8 10 9 7 5 3 1

Published in 2008 by BBC Books, an imprint of Ebury Publishing.
Ebury Publishing is a division of the Random House Group Ltd.

Doctor Who is a BBC Wales production for BBC One
Executive Producers: Russell T Davies and Julie Gardner

The Random House Group Ltd Reg. No. 954009.
Addresses for companies within the Random House Group can be found at www.randomhouse.co.uk.

A CIP catalogue record for this book is available from the British Library.

ISBN 978 1 846 07562 9

The Random House Group Limited supports the Forest Stewardship Council (FSC), the leading international forest certification organisation. All our titles that are printed on Greenpeace approved FSC certified paper carry the FSC logo. Our paper procurement policy can be found at www.rbooks.co.uk/environment

Series Consultant: Justin Richards
Project Editor: Steve Tribe
Cover design by Lee Binding © BBC 2008

Typeset in Albertina and Deviant Strain
Printed and bound in Germany by GGP Media GmbH, Poessneck

To John, Lesley, Jo, Katie and Brie – the Parkins

Sea-green waves broke against the white sand of the beach then crawled away again, before crashing back. If anyone had been on the beach, they could have stared out to sea, listened to the waves and thought that this was an untroubled place.

Then a new noise, a bit like the crash of the waves at first, but soon louder and more discordant, until it sounded like a couple of elephants competitively clearing their throats. A pure white light began flashing three metres in the air, and slowly a solid blue shape filled in beneath it. After a few seconds, rows of square panels were visible. By the time the strange sound had died away and the writing on one of the wood panels and over the doors was legible, the TARDIS had arrived.

The first thing the Doctor noticed as he stepped out was that the sky here was as green as Earth's sky was blue. Which was a nice change, he thought. Although really all it meant was that there was a lot of water vapour in the atmosphere. He was itching to tell someone you got green skies on Earth, but only when a tornado was on its way. And that this was a planet nestled deep in Galaxy Seven, or the Sculptor Dwarf Galaxy as it had been known on the old charts until the tourist board had changed it. And that, because they were almost exactly 290,000 light years from Earth, and because it was almost exactly the year 292,009, if they had a really powerful telescope they could look through it and see the Earth in the year 2009.

But there was no one with him to tell.

The Doctor had travelled alone before, often for decades at a time. After the Time War, when he'd lost everything but his TARDIS, he had decided he didn't need companions or friends. Then he'd met Rose, who had been both those things and so much more. He'd vowed to travel alone after he lost her... Well, that hadn't lasted, and quite right too.

He found he was smiling, even though he was feeling a little sad.

It was late afternoon here. It was quite warm, despite a stiff, swirling breeze which tugged and flapped the hem of his long brown coat but hadn't quite decided on the direction it should blow.

The Doctor knew where he was going, though. He turned on his heel to face the ruined city.

The TARDIS had landed on the beach that marked one edge of Arcopolis. The other end of the city was over the horizon. In front of the Doctor now was a gleaming cliff made up of different apartment blocks, terraces and observation needles, all built to jostle for a view of the sea, tetrised together, blocking out the rest of the city, except for the odd tower and spire that peeked over.

The Doctor set off up the wide, empty beach. The sand had been scrubbed clean of almost all evidence that people had come down here to sunbathe, build sandcastles, read bad books and go on donkey rides. The beach was broken up by rows of metal posts leading into the sea, all that was left of structures that once must have been windbreaks, boardwalks and piers. The metal was corroded, badly in places. The saltwater would have got into the joints. Sand had drifted up and half-covered everything.

Against the walls, there were the old ways into the city: antigrav tubes, lift shafts and sliding doors – all blocked off and useless now. The Doctor went up to one set of heavy doors, but it was no good: they wouldn't budge. He followed the wall along, knowing he'd find a way in eventually. Ten minutes later, he came to a spiral staircase that led up a couple of levels. He climbed it, found he was facing a large round window which hadn't been smashed in a storm or even cracked, but had stood there, resolute, for fifteen summers and winters.

The Doctor rectified that. He pointed the sonic screwdriver at the glass, which crazed and rained down. Careful not to cut himself, the Doctor eased into the apartment. The room was large. Comfortable modular sofas faced the window and the shore. There was an auto-dispenser table with chairs around it. A cleaning robot sat in the middle of the floor, its batteries worn down. A couple of paintings were beginning to fade and there were occasional streaks of rust on the walls. There was a musty smell, already beginning to swirl away now the Doctor had let fresh air in.

He walked through the apartment. The decor lacked soul, he thought. Monochromes and metal and dark glass, every line and curve had been calculated to five decimal places.

There was no sound except the sea, and it was a long way away. The Doctor was at the back wall now, where another large window gave a panoramic view of the city of Arcopolis.

Many civilisations, if they lasted long enough, reached the stage the builders of Arcopolis had. Such peaceful and prosperous civilisations perfected the art of designing cities, building incredible metropolises, with beautiful buildings that housed uncountable numbers of people. The most wonderful places to live: clean and busy, exciting and quiet, diverse and safe, vibrant and private, planned but friendly.

The buildings of Arcopolis were made from miracle materials that could be as tall as you wanted, and any shape at all, so the skyline was made up of towers, spheres, corkscrew pinnacles, domes perched on tiny columns, crystal pyramids and complicated combinations of all those and more. All of them were sheer, smooth and gleaming, metal and glass and plastic and ceramics. The view from the window was of thousands of such buildings, and the walkways and metal roads which connected them. There were great big spires on the top of every building.

No people, though, not any more. Once there had been many millions of people here. Now, there was no one, not a single soul. You could hear it – or rather not hear it. You could see it, too. There was no traffic running along the overpasses or through the air. Although the skyline was mostly intact, and although this was still a beautiful place, if you looked closely at the buildings you could see the consequences of neglect. Cracked and missing windows. Water run-off had formed grooves and channels of rust down the roofs and sides of buildings. Some of the walkways and travel tubes had fallen away from their moorings and were now swinging lazily in the breeze. One nearby bridge visibly swayed, half its cables snapped. Ivy, or something very like it, was beginning to claim the skyscrapers. There had been fires. The flat saucer at the top of the nearest needle was charred and cracked. Other towers and structures had been reduced to ribs of blackened metal or piles of rubble. The fires weren't the result of a war, at least not directly. Without people looking after the place, power lines would have ruptured, lightning would have struck.

A few miles away, right at the heart of Arcopolis, glimpsed among the native buildings like a wolf in a forest, was the reason no one lived here any more.

The Fortress.

A solid black pyramid, squared off, its summit the highest point in the city, twice as high as anything else. It was obviously alien, out of place. There was nothing else in Arcopolis that had those sharp angles and brutal black spikes, nothing else there was *ugly*. It radiated evil and, even from a distance, it was possible to make out the guns that bristled on the ramparts and turrets.

The Fortress was as lifeless as the rest of the planet. Even so, there would be automatic defences, death traps, nasty little surprises left posthumously by those who had built it. You'd have to be barmy to go anywhere near the place. Barking. Off your chump *and* your rocker. A complete wally.

The Doctor estimated that, on foot, it was going to take him about three hours to get there.

Back on the beach, the TARDIS sat, sunk a little – not too much – into the soft, wet sand.

A hand reached out, touched the painted wood of the police box's door. One of its six fingers traced the shapes of the letters on the sign for a few moments.

The hand was transparent, ghostly.

It reached for the door handle.

PART ONE
THE EYES OF A CHILD

ONE

The first walkway the Doctor tried almost gave way beneath his feet. The second creaked disconcertingly, and he half-ran, half-tiptoed across it. He didn't even dare put his foot on the third. He'd got two city blocks closer to his goal and decided to enter the nearest tower and descend to ground level – an easier task than he'd dared hope, as the building had a fantastically carpeted staircase. This place had been a hotel. The robot porters and janitors were all gathered by a large recharging station just off the lobby, puzzled expressions permanently stuck on their mechanical faces. Like their human masters, who they'd clearly survived, they'd have taken the power supply for granted.

There was a garage, full of speeders and flyers and one- or two-man flying saucers. The Doctor had toyed with the idea of just fixing an aircar up and driving the rest of the way but, with each one he found, a lot of the mechanics had rusted or rotted away, and the power cells were dead.

He'd quickly decided he could walk to the Fortress in half the time it would take to fix one up. The exercise would do him good.

The Doctor wished he could have just flown the TARDIS there, but that would have been a very, very bad idea. He'd landed as close as he dared.

The ground here was metal, a broken-down moving pavement. It was littered with rubble, shards of glass and scrap metal – chunks of material that had fallen from the surrounding buildings after winter storms or as whatever held them up there corroded away. There was a raised monorail line that ran straight and in roughly the direction of the Fortress. The Doctor clambered up. The line itself was in a bad way. Metal expanded when it was hot, contracted when it was cold, and engineers had to allow for that by leaving gaps at intervals in the rails, or they'd crack or buckle. When trains ran over those gaps, they made that 'clickety-clack' noise, the whole universe over. The trick was to keep the gaps clean, or they'd fill up with leaves and rust.

The city had been carefully designed so that sunlight streamed over every building and down to every level. Even at ground level it was still bright. The sun was low in that green sky now, though. All that light meant weeds and grass had thrived, poked through holes in the concrete, making the monorail line a thin strip of green life that warmed the Doctor's hearts. There were even a few scattered saplings that would be great trees, given a few decades. Something on this planet had survived the cataclysm, and in the long term that was all that needed to. Three hundred million years from now, this city would be a thin, silvery geological layer in the rock, and some distant descendant of these weeds would have evolved to puzzle over it. Earth had seen similar turmoil and mass extinction before humans had come along.

Perhaps tomorrow the Doctor would take the TARDIS into the far future, have a wander round that civilisation. Pop in for a chat with a weedy geologist.

The Doctor stopped, turned. Something had caught his eye as he walked past it. Behind him, in the mud, was a footprint.

He bent down and put on his glasses. He soon found a short line of footprints in a thin patch of dirt. Human, near enough. Whoever had made them had six toes on each foot, certainly, but they were bipedal, they didn't have hooves or paws or caterpillar tracks. The foot was a Size 9, the Doctor estimated. Not that this person had been wearing shoes. Barefoot. No evidence he – or she – had cut their feet on the metal or glass, though, as the Doctor surely would have done if he hadn't had his trainers on.

Pacing it out, like the page of Good King Wenceslas, marking the footsteps, the Doctor decided they'd been made by a person a little shorter than him, who had been walking, not running. The prints were in thin mud, so it wasn't possible to estimate the weight of the person who'd made them. They were fresh – an hour old, at the most. He hadn't anticipated anyone else being here. The implications of having company were all worrying.

The Doctor took his glasses off and looked around. There was a figure at ground level, ducking round a corner, out of sight. Even the Doctor hadn't had much time to take it in.

The Doctor clambered down to where the movement had been, but it wasn't there now.

A pile of burned-out aircars blocked the other end of this passage. The Doctor looked straight up at the perfectly smooth, vertical sides of hundred-storey buildings. It was hard to see how anyone could have got away. At ground level, there were small niches and crevices in the walls, but nothing even he could squeeze into, and he was notoriously skinny. It must have been a trick of the light. It wouldn't even qualify as a particularly good trick. And he *was* on edge. The Doctor concluded that there hadn't been anyth—

A dark shape leapt out at the Doctor; he turned to face it and was almost blinded. Belatedly, he realised the attacker had the sun behind it. By then, the creature was on him, shoving him over with a plank of wood.

'Ghost!' a high-pitched voice yelled out.

'Don't let a ghost touch you!'

The Doctor hadn't quite been knocked off his feet, and his vision was quickly returning to normal. Now the walls were coming alive, with over half a dozen other shapes rushing out from the cracks and gaps.

They were children, the Doctor realised. None of them looked more than about 12. Boys, mostly, all dressed the same sort of way, in very smart dark outfits which were all a bit too baggy, but brightly decorated with bits of colourful foil and plastic ribbon. The children each carried two or three small bags which clanked and rattled as they moved. They looked human, or close enough. They were all rather pale.

'He's a ghost,' one of the boys called.

'Looks like we got ourselves a ghost,' another agreed.

'I'm not a ghost,' he laughed. 'I'm the Doctor and this is—' He turned and then looked back, sheepish. 'No one.'

'Who were you talking about?'

'Just force of habit.'

'You know what I think? I think we are… we *is* talking to a ghost.'

'You were right the first time,' the Doctor said helpfully. '"You *are* talking to a ghost".'

'He says *he's* a ghost!'

'Ghost. Ghost. Ghost,' all but one of them started chanting.

The boldest of the boys was advancing, swinging a piece of metal pipe. The Doctor blocked it, elbowed the pipe out of the boy's hand. The boy was wiry, but he was also only 10 years old. Strong for his age, but not much of a threat. Another child – it wasn't the Doctor's top priority to work out if it was a boy or a girl – was already lunging with a very fancy-looking knife. The Doctor stepped out of the way, tripped the child up and found himself shoving over a boy with a piece of brick in his hand.

After that, the children stopped the attack and started circling. They'd moved around so they'd blocked the only escape route from the passageway. The boy who'd attacked first retrieved his metal pipe. They were still shouting out 'ghost, ghost, ghost' over and over. The Doctor didn't feel any safer, and the children were clearly preparing to pounce. Every so often one of them would step forward, quickly withdrawing. They were testing him, like a pack of animals would.

A stocky girl was the exception, the only one not chanting. She'd spent the time standing there looking thoughtful. The Doctor decided to concentrate on her.

'A ghost?' he said, addressing her directly. 'Ridiculous. You can see right through that explanation, right? See through it? Ghost.'

She was glaring at him. The Doctor's face fell.

'Loses a bit in translation, probably. Jokes tend to. Point is: I'm sure you can convince your friends here that I'm not a ghost.'

'Ghosts don't bleed,' she said. 'We could see if you bleed.'

The Doctor nodded slowly, pursed his lips. 'Well, yes, I suppose that's an example of the scientific method.'

'We should cut you open,' the boy with the fancy knife leered.

'Do you see a lot of ghosts?' the Doctor asked, suddenly. A thought had struck him. 'You don't happen to have six toes, do you? Any of you? You're not barefoot. All wearing very nice shoes. They look brand new.' A brainwave struck him, and he pointed down at his own feet. 'Trainers. Look. Teenagers love trainers, right? These are a bit big for you, of course. But if you'd like them, I'm sure we can come to some arrangement. If this is a mugging, that is.'

'A what?' the lead one asked.

'If you're mugging me for my shoes.'

'Why would we do that?'

'Don't you like my shoes?' The Doctor felt insulted.

'Who are you?' the stocky girl asked. She was tallest, and she looked stronger than most of the boys. Girls tended to at that age. The lad with the metal pipe looked like the leader, though.

The Doctor decided to assert some authority. He gritted his teeth and pulled out his psychic paper, opening up the wallet and swinging it round so that he was sure all the kids could see it.

'What's that?' the leader asked.

'It's got writing on it,' the stocky girl replied.

'Yes, that's right,' the Doctor said patiently.

'Writing?' echoed another one of them, a particularly grubby boy who looked about 12.

The Doctor held it steady, up in front of that child's eyes.

'We don't *read*,' the boy said dismissively. 'No one *reads*.'

'Ah. Well, it says –' the Doctor checked it, '– that I'm from the planet Ofsted and… Ofsted. That's, oh… Well, take my word for it, that's funny. You clearly don't think so. Fair enough. It's that joke/translation thing again.'

The kids were all glaring at him.

The Doctor grimaced as he put the wallet back in his pocket. 'Anyway, if you could just… How many of you are there, by the way? Not here in this alley. There are eight of you here. How many people live here?'

Again, it was only the girl who was listening to him. The grubby boy was at her side, though, hands in his pockets, and it really looked like he was waiting for her lead. This still meant there were half a dozen others to worry about.

'Maybe he knows about ghosts,' the grubby boy suggested.

'Oh, I've met ghosts in my time,' the Doctor said cheerfully.

The wrong thing to say. The others were nervous, now.

'Ghosts aren't the spirits of the dead or lost souls,' he said firmly, like he was teaching an unruly class. 'Ghosts are usually a sign that there's a discontinuity in the space-time continuum. Nothing to worry about. Just the sort of thing that happens. Five times out of five. Guaranteed. Well… unless they're Gelth. Or time travellers with a dodgy temporal feedback circuit. Or from the future of an alternative timeline. Or an osmic projection. Or it might be because this city was built over a time rift.'

He hesitated, because he'd run out of fingers. 'Or they could be holograms. Or waterhive. Or an army of millions of Cybermen from a parallel universe. OK… that's eight. Eight out of, er, five. Let's call it ten. So… two times out of ten, a ghost is—'

A brick sailed past him, clattered and clanged against the metal wall. The Doctor sensed he was losing his audience.

'Thing is, there's always a rational explanation,' he said calmly, but quickly. 'A reason. If you've got a ghost problem… well, I'm your man. Ghosts, I can help with.'

'He helps ghosts!' another of the boys shouted.

'Um… that's not quite what I—'

'He said he was the reason for the ghosts.'

'He called himself the Ghost Doctor.'

'That he knows eight different types of ghost.'

'He said five.'

'He said ten.'

'He said nine,' the stocky girl corrected them.

'You're right – I said nine,' said the Doctor. 'But you're missing the nuances—'

'What's the ghost talking about now?' The boy with the metal pipe was slapping it in the palm of his hand.

'What's a new onz, then? Is that the type of ghost you are?'

'He's not a ghost. He helps them and he talks to them,' the stocky girl reminded the crowd.

The children's reaction made it clear they didn't see this as an improvement.

'Doesn't matter what,' dismissed one of them.

'I think I saw a ghost here a minute ago,' the Doctor told her, almost pleading for calm. 'Now... I'm new here. Only just arrived and—'

Another rock flew past.

'I wish I could see a ghost,' the Doctor said.

That seemed to shut them up.

'No!' the one with the fancy knife shouted.

'He wished it!'

One of the boys screamed.

'You heard him! He summoned it. You saw it.'

'It?'

'The ghost.' The grubby boy was jabbing a finger at the Doctor. No: jabbing it to indicate something behind him. The Doctor took a deep breath before bowing to the inevitable and turning to take a look.

The ghost shimmered. Its features were blurred and difficult to make out. It was a man, or the shape and size of one. It wore white robes, a toga, and was terrifying because it looked so terrified. It was an expression that the Doctor recognised, but could never get used to. His instinct was to run, and he fought it, beat it down, kept himself rooted to the spot. He was looking at a man who knew that he'd lost everything, absolutely everything he knew and loved, including all the things he thought would be there for ever, all the things that should have survived him. And the Doctor could tell that, once, this had been a man, a confident, proud man, who thought he had achieved and built and protected those things he valued. A good man reduced to a lost soul. He stared at the Doctor with accusing eyes.

'I know,' the Doctor said.

The ghost reached out with both hands, trying to grab at the Doctor, just looking for one last moment of contact, some way of bridging the gap.

'I know,' the Doctor repeated, raising his hand.

'Don't let it touch you!' the boy with the metal pipe shouted. The ghost swept his arm around, almost casually, touched the boy, who vanished, his screams abruptly cut off. The metal pipe clattered to the ground.

'Frad! No!' the grubby boy said, grabbing the pipe. There wasn't much room between them. The ghost turned to face him, pleading. The ghost was fading away. It was already hard to make out where it ended and the air started.

'No...' the boy shouted, but it was too late, and the ghost swept towards him, looked almost apologetic. The boy was wild-eyed.

'Let go of him!' the Doctor shouted.

This had the intended reaction – the ghost was distracted, turned away from the boy. The stocky girl pulled him away.

The kids were all running off, now, out of the alley into the open. A couple of them were still screaming.

'Class dismissed,' the Doctor whispered.

The Doctor looked back at the ghost, unsure whether to feel anger. The ghost was hardly there, now. It looked confused. It howled, but didn't even have the power to break the silence. And then it dissipated, losing even itself.

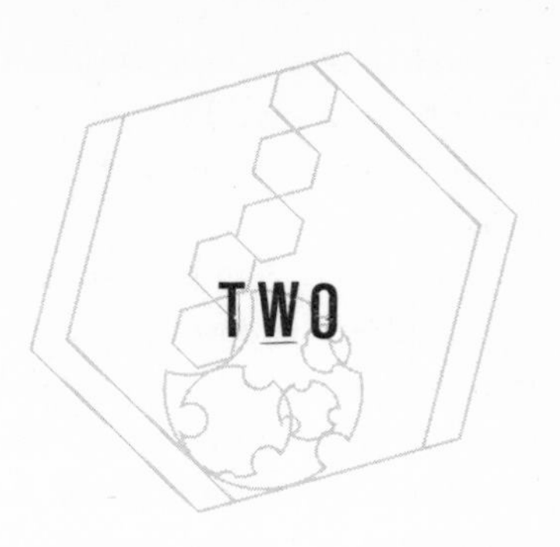

TWO

The children ran away and kept running until the first few of them couldn't run any further. They regrouped, gathered in a place they knew well, the Metal Room. Big and square, it was at the base of one of the tallest towers. It made them feel safe, because it took four of them to push the door open and closed. It never closed all the way, because for some reason the sides had great fist-thick metal rods embedded in them.

The room contained something really valuable: little strips of paper, printed with pictures of people and buildings and number symbols. If you held the paper up to the light, you could see other faces trapped in there. One of the oldest kids, Joss, had once said those were ghosts, and everyone laughed at him and called it joss paper from then on. The paper burned really well, kept them warm. There were also neat piles of shiny yellow metal bars and great tubs of bagged-up metal discs. They were no good for burning and just got in the way.

The older, fitter kids still had some energy, and they kept watch. They all knew that the ghosts never followed them, but they were still shaken up. Frad had been popular. They'd go back to the alley later, and lay a floral. What none of the kids knew was what had happened to the skinny grown-up in the odd brown coat. This didn't stop them speculating, and opinion ranged from him being the man that had been summoning up the ghosts all these years, right through to imagining that the ghost they'd seen ate the man after they ran off. Soon, everyone was arguing about the Ghost Doctor.

The stocky girl was clever enough to understand that she couldn't explain who the man was. The idea that there was a person she didn't know disturbed her. She listened to the bragging for a few minutes before it began annoying her so much she had to slip outside.

She got her thoughts straight, tried to separate out what she'd seen for herself from the confusion and rumour. They were getting silly in there, treating it like a game. They were kids. If she was thinking like that – and she'd been thinking like it for months – it meant she was growing up. She fought the next thought, tried to keep it quiet, but still it came: *there's no choice, it's nearly time to go back.*

The Ghost Doctor was too important for kids to deal with. Too big for games. Boy games *or* parent games. She fished around in her bag, found what she was looking for right at the bottom.

It had been months since she'd last seen the comm, and during that time it had got a long, annoying scratch down its screen.

She swirled one of the controls and it bleeped to let her know she was being connected. It was a whole minute before Professor Jeffip answered. A tiny hologram of him appeared, hovering over the top surface.

'Alsa… are you in trouble?' he began.

'No. Frad was taken by a ghost, but—'

'This is for emergencies,' he chided her, turning away. 'Real emergencies. The batteries, Alsa. The batteries.'

Despite herself, she was guiltily imagining the electricity seeping away like sand from an hourglass. 'There's a… man we don't know here.'

Jeffip scowled. 'You must be upset, but that's no excuse for making up stories—'

'I'm not,' she snapped. 'It's true. He's not a ghost, he's a…'

'Stranger,' he said, supplying a word that Alsa only dimly knew and had never spoken.

'*Stranger.*' She rolled the word around her mouth. 'Yes. We cornered him, and then a ghost appeared and we ran off. I think he might have summoned up the ghost, but I'm not sure. He asked stupid questions, like whether we had six toes.'

Professor Jeffip believed her. He knew she wouldn't dare waste the comm if she was making up a story. He wasn't treating her like a kid. Alsa liked that.

'Describe him,' he said.

'Tall. Thin. He was old, but not as old as you. He said he was called "the Doctor", but that's not a proper name, is it? His clothes looked… made but not new. Not torn or dirty or anything, just…'

'See what he's up to. See if there's anyone with him. Use the comm to take pictures of him and send them here.'

'The batteries...' Alsa said.

'I know, but this is important.'

Alsa hesitated.

'Who do you think he is?' she asked.

'I don't know. I might if I see his picture.'

'Do you think it was him who murdered Jall?'

'Jall was frightened to death by a ghost.'

'She wasn't,' Alsa hissed. 'I heard she was—'

'Don't start that again, Alsa. Look... this Doctor sounds dangerous. Stay careful, Alsa. It's good to hear from you.'

The hologram faded away, and the tiny device powered down. That had been the longest comm call Alsa could remember.

Alsa stood, ready to go. Gar had come out. He was always so dirty. They were the same age, and he'd always been taller than her until this year. He hadn't grown for ages, and she'd done nothing but. It felt like she was twice his size. He never took his hands out of his pockets. That had never bothered Alsa before – these days it did nothing but bother her.

'Where are you going?' he said, his voice a little whiny.

'I've commed Professor Jeffip. Told him about the *stranger*. He wants me to follow.' She started walking, soon passing the Blue Pyramid.

Gar looked confused, and trailed after her. 'You told on us? You told them where we are?'

'No. I told Professor Jeffip about the Doctor and his ghost. It's important, Gar.'

'So's not telling.'

'This is more important. Bigger.'

'Is he part of your plan?' he asked, half-cheekily, half-respectfully.

'How could he be? I didn't know about him.'

'Thought you knew everything.'

'I'll hit you in a minute.'

They picked their way over a large pile of metal slabs. They had obviously once all fitted together to make a building. It must have blown over. Or perhaps some other kids had vandalised it. There was no better route round, but climbing over the metal involved a lot of sliding, and every time they put a foot down it made a clanging sound. At the top of the pile, Alsa took the opportunity of a good vantage point to take a look around. Then she skidded down, back to ground level, Gar close behind, almost losing his footing – and his foot – in the attempt.

'The Ghost Doctor was good at fighting,' he said when he was back on level ground.

Alsa frowned. 'He wasn't. He was nearly killed by a bunch of kids.'

'That's not what happened, is it? Everyone tried to get him, but no one even touched him.'

She hadn't thought of it like that. 'If he was good at fighting, he'd have hit back,' she said, finally, unsure of her argument.

There was a mid-level golden walkway close by, and they took the pedestrian ramp about a dozen levels up to it.

Alsa was already drawing up a plan. 'We know he was

by Car Wall, but not where he's heading. Stay up here and we'll get a good view of him.'

'If he's still on ground level.'

'If the Ghost Doctor doesn't live here, he won't know the best routes.'

'I don't get it. Only kids explore. He's a parent.'

'He's not, he just looks like one. All we need to worry about is that he's dangerous.'

'We need to make sure he doesn't see us.'

'Oh, I saw you when you were by that blue pyramid,' a man's voice said.

Alsa and Gar whirled round. The Doctor was standing there.

For a while, the Doctor had stood in the alleyway, staring at where the ghost had been. He'd tried waving the sonic screwdriver around to see if it could detect anything. He knew the ghost was dead and gone. Even more dead and gone than normal for a ghost. In the end, he'd concluded there just weren't any clues there for him. The Doctor had his suspicions, but he'd decided not to worry about it for the time being.

The three hours he'd estimated it would take to get to the Fortress looked absurdly optimistic. He'd barely got half a mile in the first hour. He knew he'd be hard pushed to get to the Fortress before dark. Added to that was the fact that Arcopolis was busier than he'd anticipated. With ghosts and feral – if very well-dressed – kids around, the sooner he could get to the Fortress and concentrate on the job at hand the better.

The Doctor passed another gang of children, or perhaps two gangs, playing with a cylindrical ball that players would occasionally just grab and use as a club. Most of them were boys; they were all in their early teens. He gave them a wide berth, and they were too busy with their game to spot him.

Soon after, he'd seen two of the children who'd attacked him – the grubby boy and the stocky girl. They were looking for him, and after a little while, he'd decided to show himself.

'Hello again.' He was grinning. 'If you're going to back away from me, watch out for that drop behind you. No handrail. Common design problem in megacities across the universe, I've found. I'm the Doctor, by the way. Didn't catch your names before.'

If he set a ghost on her, Alsa knew she wouldn't be able to get away. She'd already decided she would throw herself from the walkway instead.

'Gar,' said Gar.

'Alsa,' Alsa found herself answering. 'How did you get up here so quickly?'

'Ah, well, trick of the trade. I've been doing this sort of thing a very, very long time.'

'You a doctor?'

'Yes, that's right.'

'Anossticktrishian?'

'Obstetrician?'

'Yeah.'

'No. Well, not really. I dabble.'

'Did you kill Jall?'

'No.'

Alsa knew he was telling the truth, because he hadn't hesitated, hadn't pretended, he'd just answered. He looked a little sad, added he didn't know about Jall and asked them to tell him about her.

Alsa was wary, but Gar had already started. 'She was a girl. Fair hair. They found her body a couple of days ago. The parents say she died of fright because she went where she wasn't meant to.'

Alsa narrowed her eyes. 'What are you doing here?'

The Doctor pointed. 'Heading to the Fortress.'

Alsa gasped. Beside her, she swore Gar was swaying. Perhaps it was her.

'You can't,' Gar said firmly. 'No one's allowed there. Kids or the parents. No one would *want* to go there.'

'So… it's a forbidden zone,' he said.

Alsa frowned. 'A what? It's just the Fortress, that's all. It's the way it is.' She crossed her arms over her chest. 'We've told you everything we know,' she said curtly. 'Even those of us who come to the city don't go to… that place. We just don't.'

'You didn't build it, did you?'

'Of course I didn't build it, I'm just a kid.'

The Doctor laughed. 'Not you personally. Your people. Your parents' people.'

'No,' admitted Alsa. 'It happened before we was born. Fifteen years ago. It just appeared one morning. If you go to one of the towers nearby or the Car Factory you can see the half-buildings.'

The Doctor nodded thoughtfully. 'Everything in the space the Fortress materialised into would have been destroyed. Anything that wasn't would have been unaffected. So there are buildings that were sliced in two. The half-buildings. Fascinating.'

'No one knew what the Fortress was or where it was from or why. They tried investigating, but still didn't know. Then three days later everyone vanished. Everyone but the parents. They were all in the same travel tube. It broke down, and they dug their way out and when they got there everyone was gone. Just vanished, and something had been done to the jennraters and puters and fabs so they didn't work any more.'

'All the birds and fish and animals went, too,' Gar said. 'I've seen pictures of them, though.'

'The plants survived,' the Doctor said.

'The parents would have starved otherwise,' Alsa said.

'How many parents are there?'

'All of them,' Gar replied, puzzled.

'Thirty-seven,' Alsa told the Doctor.

'Why do you think it happened?' he asked.

'The parents argue about that. No one knows. Especially the ones who say they do know.'

The Doctor was looking at Alsa, intently, but when she faced him, he looked away suddenly and guiltily.

'We did something wrong, didn't we?' Gar said. 'We was punished.'

'You were punished all right,' the Doctor said quietly. 'But not for anything you did. You certainly didn't do anything wrong. You weren't even born.'

'You know what happened?' Alsa asked him.

The Doctor smiled gently and got up. 'I'm going to the Fortress. It's going to be very dangerous.

'You can't get inside. There's no doors.'

'There are if you know where to look.'

'People who go there get struck by lightning.'

'Bet they do. That's why your parents are right, and you have to stay away.'

'Can I take your picture with my comm?' Alsa said suddenly.

'Um... yes. I suppose.'

The Doctor quickly ran his fingers through his hair and then watched – with a rather fixed grin the whole time – as Alsa took the device out, waggled the control and made a hologram of him.

'You said there was no power after everyone vanished,' he said through his teeth. 'How does that run?'

'Batteries,' she said simply. 'You can't waste them.'

'May I?' She handed it him. He'd finally stopped grinning. 'And this is a "comm", so – what? – that's short for communicator? You can talk to people with this, too? So your parents have managed to set up a telephone network?'

'It's my mum, Olva, that keeps it running,' Gar said proudly. 'There's big batteries and one aerial in town. It's for emergencies.'

'Good for her,' the Doctor said cheerfully. He stood up from the bench then looked over the edge. 'Ooh! What's that?' he asked.

Gar and Alsa ran past him to take a look. They didn't

see anything, and when they turned back to challenge the Doctor he'd vanished.

'We need to call Professor Jeffip again,' Alsa said. She didn't like to admit it.

'What with?' Gar said. 'He's nicked your comm.'

THREE

The sonic screwdriver had its limits. Not many, but it wasn't just a magic wand. Using it, the Doctor could fiddle around and make a piece of equipment run a little faster or give it more range, but it couldn't easily turn a toaster into a CD player or a lawnmower into an electric toothbrush.

Take Alsa's comm (as, indeed, the Doctor just had). It was a mobile phone. There came a point where there was no point making a phone any smaller or lighter, or its memory any bigger, or giving its camera any more megapixels. There were only so many human emotions in need of emoticons to express them. This was a nice piece of technology. It was easy to use, with all sorts of foldy-outy, 3D, pluggy-inny things down the sides. Once it had topped up the comm's battery and buffed out the scratch on the screen, there wasn't all that much else that the sonic screwdriver could add or enhance.

The Doctor had been more interested in what it could

tell him. There had been a slim hope that the city datanet was still around, or that bits of it were. But, no, there was nothing but that one mast that Gar's mum was in charge of. You could have the most brilliant device for accessing the internet going, but if there was no internet it wasn't much use.

He had thought all that through without slowing his pace. He was now back on target, and the Fortress was so close that it had started to loom. The evening light seemed to fall into the Fortress, unable to escape. He'd be at those black metal walls in half an hour.

The terrain had changed. A sewer main or railway tunnel had caved in, leaving a wide, tile-lined river. Plants had thrived, and all sorts of reeds and mosses proliferated in, beside and along the banks. The air was thick with pollen. The water was slow-flowing, and really rather a pleasant surprise, like finding a nice canal path while walking around a busy city centre. Everything was clean, as you'd expect it to be after fifteen years of cleansing rains. The ground was nicely squishy under his feet.

The Doctor passed through an archway formed by two small buildings, one on each bank, that had toppled and half-collapsed into each other—

—and suddenly there was nothing between him and the Fortress.

It felt as if it had jumped out at him, and the Doctor edged back under the concrete arch, keen to get out of its sight. He peeked round the corner and – careful to give himself as much cover as possible – got a good view. He quickly understood how the Fortress had managed to sneak up.

The collapsed and sunken buildings had formed a series of dams and terraces, and, over the years, the water had collected, overflowed, built up, until a large artificial lake had formed. It was a clearing in the forest of skyscrapers, space needles, pylons and towers.

One side of the Fortress was facing full on to the lake, the other two were swept back and partially embedded in a huge, curving white building. Smaller towers and needles – each one as large as any that had ever been built on Earth – lay around the Fortress, like felled redwood trees. The lines of the Fortress were broken up with buttresses, battlements, odd jutting features that might have been watchtowers. Plates of metal seemed to have been bolted on, carelessly at times, to reinforce the structure. There weren't any obvious windows or hatches.

The lake was a mile wide, easily. Every so often, nowhere near enough to provide a set of stepping stones, masonry and metal fins broke the surface of the water. The far shore was lapping against the solid black Fortress wall. An accidental moat. The Doctor hadn't thought to bring a canoe with him. He stood quietly on the shore, looking for a route across.

About halfway across the water, a glass man stood. The figure was small and transparent, difficult to see. Ghostly. The Doctor thought it might be a statue – an Antony Gormley, not a Michelangelo. Some instinct, though, told him it was alive.

He spent a second or two trying to work out if it had its feet on a ruin, or simply on the surface of the lake. It was facing away from him, best as he could tell.

This ghost didn't look anything like the other one.

'Two types of ghost?' he whispered. Then, waving his arms, he called, 'Hey! You there! Hello! I'm the Doctor!'

A bolt of blue energy streaked low across the water, right at him.

This sort of thing had happened plenty of times to the Doctor before in his travels around time and space. One of the reasons he had lasted as long as 900 years was that he was always half-expecting something to start shooting at him. He was back behind cover before the ray was hitting the concrete and making a very credible attempt at shattering it.

The Doctor knelt with his back to the wall, which was warm now and still ringing from the impact. Had the glass man fired at him, or had something from the Fortress fired at the glass man and missed?

There was screaming and shouting from back the way he'd come. Children screaming. Alsa and Gar.

The Doctor extricated himself, darting back through the archway, along the riverbank. He almost collided with Gar and, by dodging him, managed to slam right into Alsa. For a moment both he and she tottered on the edge of the river, but they managed to pull back from the brink.

'Ghosts!' Gar shouted. He was powering off, under the arch, his friend already almost overtaking him. 'Don't let a ghost touch you!'

Even now, the Doctor noted admiringly, the boy still had his hands in his pockets.

Behind them, three ghosts were floating towards the Doctor. The first type of ghost. Children, this time, who didn't look much older than Gar or Alsa. All girls, with long white hair twisted in elaborate dreadlocks. Their faces were blue-grey, their whole forms translucent. They looked surprised, more than anything. Shaken. One was holding up her hand, apparently bemused she could see through it. She had five fingers.

The Doctor was about to reach out to her when he remembered not to. He remembered something else, too. He whirled on his heel, pounded after Alsa and Gar.

'Stop!' he shouted.

Gar did; Alsa either hadn't heard or pretended she hadn't. As she reached the other side of the archway and entered the clearing, the Doctor leapt, wrapped both of his arms above her knees and pushed her and himself over, in a rough approximation of a rugby tackle.

Alsa's arms flailed out, her hands actually splashing into the water.

'Gerroff...' she spat, trying to kick free.

A bolt of blue energy sailed less than a metre over their heads, silencing Alsa's protest. The Doctor let go and they crawled behind a low brick wall half-submerged on the edge of the water.

Gar was safe in the archway, and the Doctor called over to him to stay where he was.

'Were the ghosts following you?' the boy asked, his voice trembling.

'No,' the Doctor said, hoping he wasn't lying.

He poked his head over the wall, brought it down again very rapidly indeed, and another blue ray slammed past.

Alsa was wide-eyed, out of breath. 'No one survives

this. We shouldn't be here. Right from the start we're told that. No one comes here and lives.'

The Doctor looked right at her. She looked so much younger than before.

'How old are you, Alsa?' he asked. Get her to think about something else.

'Thirteen.' She was defensive again, her old self. Good.

She was so young. Too young to be part of this.

'Don't worry,' the Doctor said, looking her straight in the eye. 'You can trust me.'

'You stole my comm.'

The Doctor couldn't meet her eye for a moment. 'True,' he noted. He fished into his pocket and handed it back.

'You better not have broken it.'

'The opposite actually.' The Doctor was toying with the idea of poking his head up again.

Alsa examined the comm, then looked up at him, suspicious.

'It's got a full battery. That's... you can't do that.'

'I can, you know,' the Doctor said, glad of an excuse to stay put for a moment. 'It's rechargeable. The problem you have is you've got nowhere to recharge it. Arcopolis got past all the primitive power sources, like coal and oil and nuclear and solar. Cosmic energy collected by satellites and beamed down. That's what those aerials on top of all the buildings were for. No pollution, plenty for everyone. Well, cut a long story short, the satellites have gone.'

Alsa was staring up at him. This was the Doctor's first opportunity to study her strange outfit up close. Post-apocalyptic societies were meant to go all *Mad Max*, with studded leather straps holding up rags and animal skins. It was the rules. Alsa had roughly cut hair, like her mate had done it, but it was almost too clean and moussed. She was wearing perfume. Too much, and he could make out at least three different types. Not only that, she was also modelling a pinstripe trouser suit – not unlike his own, although baggier, crisper and fancier. Then she'd ruined the effect by sewing patches on it, attached ribbons, poked through badges and other adornments. Her mum must have gone spare. Alsa was wearing the sort of trainers you only get for Christmas. Nothing really fitted her all that well – she was wearing half a dozen pairs of socks so that her feet filled out the shoes. It didn't add up.

Or did it? The Doctor beamed as another piece fell into place. 'Oh, oh – yes! I see. You stole what you're wearing. Well, not stole – took from the shops.'

He thought about the vast city. All those shops with shelves full of… well, everything. They'd be full of stuff. Lots of things would fade or rot or perish – how quickly would depend on what they were made of, what they were packaged in, how much sunlight hit them, whether the roof leaked. Some things would last a lifetime. One of Alsa's gang had had that fancy knife. All of them had clothes and bags and stuff like that. Loads of loot.

'The parents disapprove,' Alsa said defiantly.

'Well, not to be critical, but you do overdo the perfume.'

'They say the city is dangerous.'

'On balance, I tend to agree.'

'They say we should learn to make things ourselves.

They're stupid – there's plenty of everything in the city.'

The Doctor nodded. 'It must be very difficult for them. You and Gar and the other kids, you've never known a different life. They did. It must haunt them. Losing everything.'

There was a flash as bright as the sun for the merest moment, annihilation so profound it stretched deep into the past and far into the future. Then Gallifrey was gone.

'They don't like to talk about what happened before,' Alsa was saying, a sneer in her voice. 'They always change the subject.'

'Well, they must have lost loved ones. I know how they... well, talking of which: how are you getting on over there, Gar?'

'I'm all right.'

The Doctor could see him, and gave him the thumbs up. That made Gar smile, and copy the gesture.

'Got your hands out of those pockets. Excellent. Right,' said the Doctor. 'Gar. Alsa. The Fortress is able to defend itself. No one's alive in there. It's all automatic. It was a place built for war, designed to function even after a massive assault. The... lightning... that's just a common or garden directed energy ray. Motion sensitive, unfortunately for us. It fires at anything that moves. There will be other guns like that, at intervals, along the walls. The ghosts are another defence mechanism. You're not going to want to go anywhere haunted, are you? So the Fortress projects scary images to frighten you away. Kills you if you stay too long. That's all the ghosts – both types... um, I think – are: holograms like your comm makes. And, if you remember, "holograms" were on my list of rational explanations for ghosts. I was right.'

'So… you do this all the time?' Alsa asked.

'Oh yes. Fight monsters, right wrongs, boldly go where no one has gone before.'

'Like every day?' Gar wondered.

'Most days,' the Doctor sighed. 'Too many adventures to tell in just one place. I forget half of them myself.'

'Tell us a secret one.'

'One no one else knows about? Um… yes.' The Doctor thought about that for a moment. 'All right, here's a good one: a couple of days ago, I was in a city called London. You won't have heard of it. It's on one of my favourite planets. You won't have heard of the Steggosians, either. Luckily, they haven't heard of you. A particularly nasty race of fascist dinosaur people.'

'What's a dinosaur?' asked Gar.

'What's a fascist?' asked Alsa.

'Well… imagine something as wide as I am tall, with scaly skin and a flat head. Big plates running down its back, spiky tail.' The Doctor did a helpful mime.

'And that's a fascist?'

'This particular one, yes. What matters is that the universe won't miss them. Twenty years ago, relatively speaking, the Steggosian home quadrant was hit by a terrible plague that destroyed their immune systems and left no survivors. The one I met had been the captain of a starship out on deep-space patrol when it happened. It drove him mad. They'd caught the plague from rats, and the captain decided to rid the universe of all mammals.'

'What's a mammal?' the children both asked.

'You are,' the Doctor assured them. 'The rest of his crew perished over the years. He ended up inside a clock tower, planning to release poison that was so lethal a single drop would have killed everyone in the country. A clock tower is—'

'We know what a clock tower is,' Alsa complained.

'There's one in the Car Factory,' Gar added.

'There's also a famous one in London.' The Doctor smiled. 'St Stephen's Tower, or the Clock Tower, but most people call it Big Ben. They'd only just finished rebuilding it, so I wasn't about to let anyone smash it up again.'

'What did you do to him?' Alsa asked.

'I tried talking to him,' the Doctor said quietly. 'He wasn't keen on the idea. We fought. He ended up losing his balance, falling sixty metres. Hit the pavement.'

'Splat!' Alsa squealed.

The Doctor's expression flickered. 'He had a very tough hide. But, yes, he died.'

Gar looked away, Alsa was thinking it through.

'Did you keep the poison?'

'No.' It was time to risk it. Very slowly, the Doctor stood up.

'Doctor!' Alsa shouted, grabbing at his sleeve.

'It's fine,' the Doctor reassured her. 'There's a trick to it. Move slowly. Motion sensitive, like I said, following a set of instructions. It's programmed to fire at things only if they move above a certain speed.'

'How fast?' said Alsa, standing up so slowly she'd have been shoved out the way by an impatient glacier.

'Faster than that,' the Doctor chided. He was literally inching backwards to the archway. 'Although I'm not sure how much faster. It's trial and error, really. Think of it as a game.'

'If we lose the game?'

'We'll be, er, blasted to pieces.'

The good thing about moving so slowly was that the Doctor had a chance to look back over the lake, see if he could spot the glass man again. He couldn't, but it was getting dark, and it had been hard enough to spot him before. He might be inching across the water towards the Fortress, not away from it. The thought was disturbing.

Now the Doctor was getting a good view of the Fortress, he could see the gun turret. It was a tube mounted low on a buttress, only a metre or so over the water. It was still pointing in their direction, twitching from time to time, impatiently. No ivy dared grow up the walls of the Fortress, he noted.

'Don't give in to the temptation to run the last bit,' the Doctor warned, as much for his own benefit as Alsa's.

The ground squelched beneath his left foot, sank away suddenly, and the Doctor almost – almost – fell over. He righted himself, sighed with relief, and with his next step was behind the concrete wall with Gar.

Alsa's wide shoulders were high, tense. She was like a cat with an arched back. She'd been facing away from the Fortress the whole time. Since the Doctor had nearly slipped, she'd become so cautious with her feet she was in danger of tripping over them.

'Relax a little, Alsa. Nearly there.'

Three more steps and she was safe, and as soon as she was safe her legs gave way and she sat down on the wet ground. The Doctor double-checked the other direction for ghosts. Alsa and Gar were talking amongst themselves, glancing his way from time to time.

'You're coming with us,' the girl announced as she got up.

'Where are we going?' Gar asked, before the Doctor could.

'Back to the parents.'

The Doctor bit his lip. 'I really have to get into that Fortress,' he said finally.

'You can get inside?'

'Yes.'

'Tell me what you're going to do.'

'There is a weapon in there, a terrible weapon. Not that ray gun, but something that's – and here comes a word that is overused, but not by me – infinitely more powerful. That weapon was used once, fifteen years ago. Do you understand what I mean?'

Alsa thought about it, but only for a second or two. 'It's what killed everyone.'

The Doctor nodded. He glanced at the sky and then looked back over at the Fortress.

'Go home to your parents, show them you're safe. Get some sleep, and tomorrow morning, I promise, the Fortress will no longer be a danger to anyone. I am going in there, I'm going to get past all the traps and I'm going to destroy that weapon once and for all. Then I'll go. Like I'd never been here.'

Night had fallen. The Fortress stood there, black against a too-black night's sky. It was a dark mountain, and seemed almost as large as the city it had imposed itself upon.

He could defeat it.

There was the faint whiff of perfume.

The Doctor turned, a smile on his face – just in time to see Alsa, arms aloft, bringing half a concrete block down on the side of his head. His knees buckled, he raised a useless hand, opened his mouth and splashed down into the muddy ground, the one-syllable question he was about to ask still on his lips.

'No,' said Alsa.

FOUR

The Doctor's eyes snapped open, and the sudden light made his very sore head even more sore. His hand explored his temple, discovered it was tightly bandaged.

'He's up,' a girl's voice – too young to be Alsa's – called out.

He was lying on something like a camp bed, wearing loose pyjama bottoms. Without moving, he established he was in a large room with walls made of translucent plastic, like a marquee. The light was sunlight, so he'd been unconscious all night. Risking a turn of the head, he couldn't be sure if this was a hospital ward, a machine shop or a laboratory.

The room seemed equally unclear on that point. There were cabinets along the walls, full of glass and plastic bottles, as well as various tools and scientific instruments. There were four other beds, all empty. Two large metal workbenches were packed with hand-lathes, drills, saws and so on. There were large packing crates dotted around the floor, stuffed with what looked like rolled-up posters or scrolls.

There were six girls in the room, all 7 or 8 years old, all in smart little lab coats. They were occupied cleaning bottles, writing up notes and other menial scientific tasks.

The Doctor swung his legs round, planted his feet on the rough stone floor.

'Professor Jeffip will want to know,' one girl said, to general agreement from the others. She slid open a door made of plastic sheeting and stepped through it.

From the quality of the light, they were going deeper into the building, not leaving it. The corridors the Doctor was led through reminded him of a traditional Japanese house, but while those were built in harmony with nature using local materials, the people here had made do with pieces of metal scaffolding instead of wood, and sheets of polythene instead of paper.

The girl who was leading him was so young and so self-consciously prim that the Doctor was unsure if she was playing or not.

'In here.'

The girl stepped aside and closed the door after the Doctor. It was a smaller room. A man in a mostly blue patchwork toga was hunched over a great wooden desk. The Doctor's coat, suit, shirt and tie were all hanging up on a rail beside the desk. The contents of his many and various pockets had been collected in a plastic tray. The man at the workbench had clamped the sonic screwdriver into a small vice, prised the case open and was peering at it.

'Be careful,' the Doctor said, intensely annoyed. 'You don't know what—'

'It's a sonic tool... a screwdriver,' the man told him airily, without looking up. 'I was just examining its acoustic accelerators.'

The man turned, belatedly removing the jeweller's eyeglass he'd had fixed into his eye. He looked like he was in his late sixties, with an aquiline noise and a high forehead. His hair was a mane that started as a quiff, ran halfway down his back and had grey streaks so dramatic they were practically stripes. His irises were different colours, one was a pale blue dot, the other a vivid red. Cinnabar, the colour of mercury oxide, thought the Doctor.

The man was toying idly with the piece of casing he'd taken off. 'We had devices like this,' he said as he did so. 'Much, much larger. The size of this room.'

The Doctor had reached the desk. He glanced down at the tray with his stuff in and, as nonchalantly as he could, confirmed the TARDIS key was there.

'Your scientific credentials are certainly impressive,' the man said, indicating the wallet containing the psychic paper. 'My name is Jeffip.'

'Professor Jeffip?'

'The children call me that, yes.'

'I'm the Doctor.'

'Yes. So Alsa's told us.' He raised his left hand, clearly the local greeting.

'Alsa...' Just hearing the name made the Doctor's head throb more.

'She and Gar brought you here.'

'She's a smart child.' The Doctor said. He'd pulled his shirt from its hanger and was slipping it back on.

'Yes. One of mine, I think. She's smart and angry. Not a terribly appealing combination.'

'No. So where's Alsa now?'

'She's not yet risen.'

'Teenagers, eh?'

'She and Gar were very tired. They brought you a long way in a wheelbarrow.'

'Did they? Did they? A wheelbarrow. Fancy that.' The Doctor whistled as he buttoned up his jacket.

'Alsa couldn't begin to explain where you had come from.'

'You've already gathered that I'm not from Arcopolis?' the Doctor ventured.

'The two hearts and pockets full of items which aren't from this planet gave it away,' Jeffip confirmed, reaching for a walking stick made from a sawn-off piece of aluminium pole. 'Would you like some breakfast?'

Jeffip's laboratory was in just one of about a dozen similar structures of various sizes and shapes. This settlement was a shanty town, albeit a rather posh one. It had been laid out in a large flat expanse of parkland at the heart of the city. It reminded the Doctor a little of Hooverville.

There were a lot of children around. A lot of them. A remarkable number. Like a dozen school trips had shown up at the same time. They were all under 10, as best he could make out. The only adult the Doctor had seen so far was Jeffip.

The pathways were festooned in bunting, paper lanterns and sculptures made of scrap metal and bits of dead robots. Anything to brighten up the place.

'Are you all right, Doctor?'

The Doctor turned to Jeffip. 'I'm sure it's nothing.'

'You look worried those robots are going to come back to life.'

The Doctor tried to sound casual. 'Stranger things have happened.'

'I wish they would. We could do with the help.'

They passed the comm mast, which stood in the middle of the settlement like a totem pole. Everyone was stopping or at least looking up as they passed. The Doctor smiled a lot, tried to look friendly.

'We always knew there must be extraterrestrial civilisations,' Jeffip was saying. 'We never made contact with any. Until the Fortress appeared. And now you, of course. How's the head?'

'It feels like something made contact with it,' the Doctor said lightly.

Jeffip nodded, smiling. 'I have many questions, of course. A few practical ones. You're here alone? Why have you come to Arcopolis? How did you know we were here and learn our language? Is that your natural form?'

'What's wrong with my form?'

'Oh, nothing. Much. It's just that it so closely resembles our own. I wondered if you'd adopted it to blend in. Like a chameleon.'

'I'm from a world that was almost identical to this one. Same size, so same gravity. Same atmosphere, just about.

Orange sky, not green. I like your sky, by the way. Don't see many green ones. Our superficial physical similarity is down to natural selection and coincidence. The same patterns repeat themselves across the universe. I'm here alone. I travel, and I've learned millions of languages on my travels. Never bothered with Welsh – didn't think I'd ever need it. Just goes to show.'

'Was?'

'I'm sorry?' The Doctor had just looked down and noticed his shoelaces were undone.

'"A world that was". Past tense.'

'You're a very perceptive man, Professor Jeffip.' The Doctor was bending down, tying his laces.

'What do you know about this world, Doctor?'

'Well…' the Doctor began, 'I know that I saw a boy killed yesterday. Touched by a ghost. I tried to save him, but couldn't. I'm sorry.'

Jeffip grunted. 'A shame. But at least it wasn't a girl.'

The Doctor let that remark go for the moment.

They were approaching running water – the Doctor could hear it. They passed through the gap between two tents and then they were on the paved bank of a very narrow, fast-flowing river. Upstream, there was a large waterwheel, fixed to the side of a brick building that had probably once only been ornamental. From the crashing and clattering coming from inside, the Doctor guessed the wheel was powering a drive shaft that, in turn, must have been running things like a small milling wheel, a loom and a lathe. Jeffip confirmed that and added that there wasn't room in there for much industry. Its main purpose was to irrigate the fields.

'You don't generate electricity?'

'Not yet. We've had other priorities.'

Set a little way from the water was a long picnic-style bench. There were three women there: a blonde, a redhead and a brunette; all of them looked around 40, perhaps a little younger. They wore similar outfits, almost like thick saris, all of them patched and mended. They were attending to a cloud of children, all under five, all with bottles of juice. Two of the women were at an advanced stage of pregnancy.

'Ladies,' said the Doctor, smiling, sitting down.

The children were, despite the women's best efforts, something of a law unto themselves.

'These aren't all yours, are they?' the Doctor joked.

'Who else's would they be?' one of them asked, too confused to be offended.

The Doctor, at the second attempt, managed to count seventeen young children. It *was* mathematically possible, he supposed.

Jeffip was dishing out a couple of bowls of soup from a large stone pot. It was watery, but looked like lemongrass and mushroom. When the Doctor tried it, it tasted surprisingly strong.

'I'm the Doctor, by the way,' the Doctor said to the one who didn't look pregnant, the one with blonde hair.

'Dela.' She raised her left hand, then returned her attention to wiping the mouth of a 2-year-old. The children all knew to drink up their soup and eat their mushrooms.

'How many children do you have? If you don't mind me asking?'

'Sixteen,' Dela told him, too busy to look up. 'I'm between at the moment.'

'Hard work,' the Doctor suggested.

Dela turned her head and raised an eyebrow.

'You knew that already,' the Doctor said.

'I knew that already,' she confirmed, giving him a nice smile.

'We have to repopulate.'

The voice belonged to a new arrival, a woman as old as Jeffip, so around 60. She was scholarly-looking, with thinning grey hair. 'Welcome to New Arcopolis. I am Jennver.'

'And do you have children?' the Doctor asked, turning away from Dela.

'Not for fifteen years,' Jennver said, without emotion.

'Ah. Yes... I understand.'

What had once been raw had been smoothed away over the years, like pebbles in a stream. Before the Fortress arrived, all of the grown-ups here would have had jobs and friends, families and an expectation of what the future was going to be like. All taken away in an instant. The Doctor wondered what they'd been like before.

'As I'm too old to have children and too weak to work the fields, I occupy myself as leader of the Council.' Jennver beamed and raised her hand.

Jeffip was smiling. 'Jennver is also our only obstetrician.'

'Delighted to meet you,' the Doctor said. This was the

first time for centuries he'd heard the word "obstetrician" twice in twenty-four hours.

'You are also a doctor,' she asked – a little warily, the Doctor thought.

'I am.'

'Alsa told me a little about you last night. The hologram she took wasn't terribly flattering.'

'She didn't get my good side,' the Doctor suggested. 'Given that it was a 3D image, that's just unforgivable. Kids, eh? You must have a terrible time controlling them. They must outnumber you ten to one.'

'They all come to understand their duty to posterity.'

'Duty?'

'Well, yes. None of us have any choices. The—'

'—women have to have lots of babies, and it doesn't matter so much if the boys are eaten by ghosts?' the Doctor finished for her. 'Either way, you don't need to teach them to read.'

The Doctor looked over to Dela for support, but she was studiously looking the other way.

Jennver bristled, but managed to stay civil. 'Our society faces exceptional circumstances, Doctor. We were left with thirteen women of childbearing age. Everyone, men and women, lost privileges and rights. None of us have the life we would ask for. We retained a functioning society. There are now 148 girls and women. The eldest of the children will soon be adults, and have children of their own. There will not be the same pressure on them.'

'I calculate that an average of ten children will suffice,' said Jeffip. 'Then six for the generation after that. We can't expand beyond the settlement's ability to feed itself, of course.'

'It is not how I would organise an ideal world,' Jennver conceded. 'We have never mistaken this situation for the ideal world. We have adopted a clan structure, one that seems to hold together.'

The Doctor nodded. His attention had wandered back to the Fortress. He needed to get on with what he'd come here to do.

The park was roughly triangular, probably two miles on each side, surrounded by skyscrapers and other huge buildings. The Fortress was visible, but further away than ever, a dark island almost lost in a sea of architecture. The Doctor was confident he could make a break for it, but he wanted as much of a head start as possible, so he was waiting for an opportunity to sneak off without alerting anyone.

They'd finished breakfast and left the mothers looking after the children. Now, an hour or so after he'd woken, the Doctor was following Jeffip and Jennver as they walked among the tents.

'I'd love to hear your thoughts on where the Fortress came from,' the Doctor told them.

Jennver looked dismissive. 'I don't think we'll ever know for sure.' She'd taken against him, the Doctor was sure of it.

The old man leant more firmly against his walking stick. 'Shouldn't stop us asking the questions, Jennver. I've been doing that for fifteen years. Certain facts are self-evident. It is the product of a civilisation far in advance of ours. That civilisation is aggressive and paranoid. They operate on a scale that I know I can't even comprehend. Their agenda is entirely unknown and their methods do not, as far as I can tell, have any precedent in our history. It is probably alien.'

'Only probably?' the Doctor asked.

'It may have time travelled from our future. In which case, it may have been built by our descendants for no other reason than that they knew it appeared when it did. The destruction of our civilisation may have been a necessary step in the creation of theirs.'

'I tend to the belief that time travel is a logical absurdity,' Jennver said.

The Doctor nodded approvingly. 'Oh, absolutely. In fact, I was saying the exact same thing to a bloke down the pub just next week.'

'They did something that wiped out 200 million people in an instant. And it obscured nine of the stars. Did you know that? I have drawn up star maps, compared them with ones from the last fifteen years.' As Jeffip said that, the Doctor remembered the box of scrolls back in his lab. 'The nine nearest stars to this world – apart from our own sun, of course. An atmospheric effect, I think.'

'Not everyone is so sure any stars have vanished,' Jennver said gently. 'None of us were even amateur astronomers.'

'Surely there are records?'

'Every database is dead, powerless.'

'There must be old books in museums and libraries?'

'We have different priorities.'

The Doctor's jaw must have dropped, because Jennver looked annoyed.

'Museums and art galleries had controlled conditions, all dependent on their power supply. We needed to plant and harvest. We couldn't afford to waste any effort.'

'So every masterpiece of all the great artists of Arcopolis is sat mouldering?'

'Rather them than the crops in the field. You can't eat books.'

Jeffip had the decency to look ashamed.

'Most of the statues and sculptures are still there,' Jeffip noted. 'We did want to bring *Dance of Days* to the settlement, make it a feature of our square, but it's solid bronze. It was just too heavy. Shame, as it's pretty inspiring.'

'It's not going anywhere,' Jennver muttered. 'We were right to start afresh.'

Jeffip was also clearly keen to change the subject. 'Doctor, we were once a proud people. We thought Arcopolis had reached the pinnacle of technology and society. But the only conclusion I can reach is that we were caught in the crossfire of some intergalactic war that had nothing whatsoever to do with us. We were an anthill run over by a tank.'

The Doctor pursed his lips, but decided not to say anything.

'Who was Jall?' the Doctor asked Jeffip later on in the morning.

Jeffip nodded, upset to hear the name. 'A lovely girl. One of the first to be born, she'd just come back to us.'

'I gather she was killed.'

'By ghosts, yes. Her body was found the day before yesterday, by the Ground Wing. It's a shame. She was old enough to start thinking about having kids of her own.'

'Alsa wanted to know if I murdered her.'

'She thought you were a ghost at first, didn't she?'

'Yes.'

'There you are, then. She's angry and she's a child, Doctor – not objective.' He hesitated. 'It's odd. So much death, but that was only the third body I'd ever seen. Everyone taken by the ghosts vanished. We lost a couple of people early on. Couldn't take it. Selfish. We've been lucky since then, in the settlement.'

That puzzled the Doctor.

It was gone midday.

Beyond the tents, the park had been ploughed up and various crops planted. The fields were full of people – children, mostly – just like pre-Industrial Revolution farms in Europe. At least on Earth they'd had horses and oxen to pull ploughs. The only mechanical sound he could hear was the splash and creak of the water wheel, on the other side of the tents.

The Doctor was keen to get back in Jennver's good books before he left. The leader of the Council was at the edge of the fields, deep in conversation with Dela.

A crowd of children – a little older than the ones he'd met at breakfast – were picking what looked like blue strawberries. A little boy offered the Doctor one, and he gratefully accepted.

'Tasty,' he said, and meant it. It actually tasted a little meaty, like beef. A little. He had another.

'So, Doctor,' Jennver said. 'You knew about the Fortress before you arrived. Did you know Arcopolis had been destroyed?'

'Yes.'

'Did you know that we had survived?' Dela asked.

'No,' the Doctor admitted.

Dela and Jennver shared a glance.

'Now you know about us, you have new plans.'

The Doctor was puzzled for a second or two, mainly because it hadn't even been a question. 'Well, yes, of course,' he said hurriedly. 'Um… what do you mean?'

'Alsa said you fixed her comm,' Dela said. 'A man of your abilities would be very useful around here.'

'Um…' He floundered for a moment. 'Oh, I see. Yes. I'm happy to do what I can to help out. I'm up for odd jobs, tinkering, fixing up. Anything, really.' He looked over at Dela and smiled. 'Within reason. Nothing that changes things too much, of course. I'm not meant to interfere, but, well, that ship sailed a long time ago.'

Jennver was smiling and nodding, keen. 'That's settled. See what you can do. We're having a Council meeting tonight. You should come to it.'

The Doctor checked his watch, looked back over at the Fortress. 'Yes, of course,' he said.

By mid afternoon the Doctor was getting itchy feet. He was a traveller, he liked travelling.

Dela was pleasant company, and now she was showing

him around, introducing him to people. She'd just had him shake hands with a brawny, bearded man called Fladon, the blacksmith, although he was away from his workshop. Fladon was in his late forties, dressed in a jumper knitted from reeds and what looked like a PVC kilt. It wasn't a look the Doctor would be rushing to adopt.

Fladon suddenly shouted: 'Come back have you?'

He was calling out to Gar, who'd just come swaggering round the corner and had his hands back in his pockets. He didn't come over, or answer Fladon's question, he was just wandering through.

'What's he doing out?' Gar scowled when he saw the Doctor. 'That's the Ghost Doctor, that is.'

'He's a man, Gar,' Dela said.

'Frad's dead,' he called out, either indifferent or successfully feigning indifference. He'd passed by, now.

'Boys will be boys,' Dela sighed, picking up a bottle Gar had dropped.

'Children shouldn't be running around outside getting exercise, they should be inside playing violent computer games and eating junk food,' the Doctor agreed.

'We let children play.'

'And die?'

'Life here is hard,' Fladon said. 'Kids learn that adults stay away from the city for good reasons. We tell them, but they have to learn for themselves, so a lot of them go out into the city when they're old enough. We give the more grown-up kids comms to use in emergencies. It's healthy to question, to work things out. They all reach the same decision in the end. Some only go there for a few days, others for years. Sooner or later, they all come back. The girls faster than the boys.'

'They all have so far,' Dela agreed quietly. 'If the ghosts don't get them.'

'And the adults never leave this park? At all?'

'Well, I remember what the city was like. It's very painful to go back, see the state it's in. All the places I went to with Gyll, just... dead.'

'Gyll?'

'Yes.' She blushed, didn't want to say any more about Gyll. 'I've not set foot there for... well, ten years. At least. Very few of us have. We've been busy here.'

'But all the stuff there...'

Fladon snorted, raised his hand to shut the Doctor up before he'd really started. 'We learned self-sufficiency. How to make things and fix things. Not rummaging around in other people's garbage.'

'That's... admirable. To an extent, but...'

'It must seem odd. Like I say, we all go through a phase of thinking that. All the kids do. But life here is fragile. Our survival is tenuous, and there's no guarantee that this place is even viable. We can't control our destiny, but we must do what we can. It's childish to think otherwise.'

The Doctor considered. 'OK... one example: medicine. Even after fifteen years, there must be medical supplies in the city that haven't expired, so do you—'

'No,' Dela said.

'All those births, you must have—'

'No,' Dela interrupted again, laughing. 'I wish we did at times.'

'Well… why don't you?'

'Because instead of relying on technology, we have to rely on ourselves.'

'Oh, too simple,' complained the Doctor. 'Too glib. Come on… when the Fortress arrived you would have both have been – what? – mid-twenties? So you know what the doctors of Arcopolis could do. So what was possible? Heart transplants – easy-peasy. Lungs, livers, kidneys… eyes. Faces. Had you done brains? They're tricky, but I bet a civilisation that could build –' he found a particularly impressive building on the skyline and pointed at it '– that skylon could manage a good old brain transplant. I bet you'd cured just about everything. If you got squished up in an aircar crash, I bet they'd just unsquishify you. I bet it was practically an outpatient's procedure.'

'We had advanced medicine,' Fladon said. 'We're certainly at an advantage now because our ancestors eliminated genetic disease. But sooner or later any medicine would run out. Better to get used to making our own remedies, rely on our own strength. Imagine what would have happened if we had been reliant on robot surgeons? I don't know what we'd have done if we hadn't had someone like Jennver who could deliver babies.'

'What's your life expectancy now, Fladon? Twenty years less than your father's?'

'At least. But the survival of the species is more important than any individual. We need to know that our grandchildren and their grandchildren will survive.'

'The ghosts keep to the city, the lightning only strikes those going near the Fortress,' Dela agreed. 'We have a life for ourselves here. It's hard, but it's safe. Take risks and we could all die.'

'It's a good way to live, here,' Fladon said.

The Doctor looked at Fladon. 'In tents, literally in the shadows of some of the most beautiful buildings ever constructed?'

'Yes. Living in the shadows is better than dying in the light.'

'We live here, now, Doctor,' Dela said softly, a little reluctantly. 'It doesn't matter what's in the city. It doesn't matter what we'd change if we could. We all of us have to learn to make the best of it.'

'Fatalism? Just letting the universe do its thing?'

'Given how we find ourselves here, how we couldn't prevent losing everything we had in an instant, it's a perfectly rational response, wouldn't you say?' Fladon said gruffly.

The Doctor stuffed his hands in his pockets and took a good look around. 'No. No, I wouldn't.'

Late afternoon, and Alsa had just got out of bed and dressed. Her limbs ached. She sat there, half-crouched, thinking about her next move. A shape shifted behind the milky plastic wall, a parent coming her way. It turned the corner, and Alsa was surprised to see the Doctor.

'I was just popping in to see Dela,' he said. 'You were on the way, so I thought I'd say "hi". Hi.'

'How's the head?' she asked, careful to sneer. Alsa realised she was sitting upright. Something about the Doctor put her on the alert.

'I had a bandage, but I took it off. There's a bruise there, but nothing worse.'

'It's so small, isn't it?'

The Doctor reached for the bruise.

'No,' Alsa said. 'This place. The settlement. All these one-storey buildings. I don't think you can even measure the tallest buildings in Arcopolis.'

The Doctor laughed. 'Well, someone had to, to build them. The tallest ones are eight, nine hundred storeys, I think, something like that.'

'You've seen taller, though?'

'On Gammadendrax, they have a tower that reaches all the way to their moon.'

'Their what?'

The Doctor spent a second considering the quickest explanation, then he said, 'It's so tall it would be like stacking all of the towers of Arcopolis one on top of each other. There's no roof, just two ground floors, one on one planet, one on another.'

'That's stupid. What happens in the middle when you're going up it? Do they start falling instead of climbing?'

'That's just what I asked. You're a very smart young woman, Alsa.' His grin melted away, and all of a sudden he looked very stern, very serious. 'Why do you behave the way you do?'

Alsa frowned. 'What choice do I have?'

'You tell me,' said the Doctor.

So she did.

Almost every kid went to the City when they were old

enough. There came a point when you just did the sums, and realised that if all the parents were busy at their work, and if there were so many more kids than adults, then there was no way the parents could stop you doing what you wanted. The very first thing every kid wanted to do was to explore the City that had been looming over the settlement all their life, utterly taboo.

Usually what happened – Alsa's experience was pretty typical – was that you'd tag along with some older kids, perhaps even break away and run back if they went too far.

Her first trip into Arcopolis, she hadn't liked it. The buildings were too tall, everything was wrong. There were shadows and tiny dangers and humiliations everywhere. She'd slipped over on a walkway and fallen into a pothole and got wet and bruised.

A lot of the girls, in particular, didn't stay there for long. They were always better looked after by the parents than the boys were, given more interesting things to do. Alsa stuck with it.

She got used to the City quickly. Soon, she was leading younger kids there herself. She'd discovered a department store once, all by herself, close to the settlement but which hadn't been touched. She'd prised open the sliding doors with a crowbar. There had been eleven kids with her, and they'd swarmed in, pushing and biting and shoving to be the first inside. They'd just run around the place in a pack at first, before breaking up into smaller groups and exploring for themselves. The store was full of everything. Clothes and make-up and sport stuff, a load of dead electronics.

There was a food hall, and that was where Alsa ended up. Most things people used to eat had been made by machines, but there were luxuries, and people got those from stores. The smell was terrible, like a cesspit. A lot of stock had just rotted. There was fruit juice, in pretty green bottles but, judging from the first half a dozen of them Alsa broke open, it had all fermented, so she left the rest alone. Some food was perfectly preserved, in plastic packs or in metal tubes. Most of the tubes had pictures of the food on.

She'd peeled back the plastic on one pack, eaten something strange, a bit like mushroom but with an odd melty, stringy texture.

'Meat,' the Doctor said.

'Eh?'

'The muscle and fat of a dead animal.'

Alsa thought about it, more curious than anything else. 'That was meat? The parents go on about meat.' She'd liked the taste, but mainly because it was so gross. She looked down at her own hand, flexed the muscles of her fingers.

'The attack wiped out all the animals. Except for the parents. Given that cannibalism is, um, off the menu, that means you're all lifelong vegetarians.'

'You've eaten meat?'

'Oh, yes.'

'You've done loads of things, haven't you?'

The Doctor pursed his lips and nodded. 'That's... fair to say. I've had more opportunities than you.'

'Yeah, well, obviously.'

'What's your plan? What's it all about, Alsa?' He sang that last bit, although she didn't recognise the tune.

'What?'

'Are you going back to the City and staying there all your life?'

'Doesn't matter what,' she said, frustrated. 'Girls become women, they get pregnant, have babies, look after them, the men help, but they can't have babies, so the women have to, so there's no choice, we need to repopulate.'

'It's your duty.'

'Are you laughing at me?'

'No.' He clearly meant it, for what that was worth.

'It's what we do.'

'But there is a choice about how you do it,' the Doctor said.

He was the first person who'd ever understood.

'They don't get angry,' she said. 'You notice that? Are they holding it all in? I can't tell. When I get angry… it boils. It never completely goes away.'

'They're not guilty, either,' the Doctor added.

'Guilty?' she said, annoyed with him. 'What have they got to be guilty about?'

'Even if you were there and saw it all, even if you know it's not your fault and you did your very best, you ask yourself why. Why did I survive? Why do I deserve to live, when so many others have died? Why was I the only one?' He paused, then, 'Guilt. Even if you hide it, it's there. It eats away at you.'

He looked up at her, gave a nervous smile.

Alsa had watched the performance, unimpressed. 'I'll

take your word for it,' she said. 'I don't feel any guilt. I wasn't there. Not my fault. But I get angry. I hate this. It's stupid. I want to lash out, hurt people. All the time. I can't help it. It's all such… it's all…'

'Wrong?' the Doctor supplied, and it was as good a word as any. 'Not the way things are meant to be. This isn't the life a 13-year-old girl should have. You've been denied so much.'

'Doesn't matter what.'

'So you keep saying. But you don't mean it, do you?'

'No one could do anything about the Fortress. Even if there had been a warning, even a hundred years' warning, what could they have done? There was nowhere to run to, no way of fighting it. We are where we are. Here in a load of stupid, small, cold plastic tents. Everything perfectly balanced by Jennver and Jeffip, no alternative, no way to change even the slightest thing without all of us dying.'

'So your solution is to lose your temper?'

She looked at him, stared him right in the eye. It was very important for him to know that this wasn't an act, this wasn't a game, this wasn't anything trivial or stupid or childish. 'Someone has to.'

The Doctor was nodding, mouth clamped shut. It was like he was grinding his teeth. Without another word, the Doctor turned and left, his coat tails flapping.

'It's all different now, though, isn't it?' she said quietly, once he'd gone. 'Now is when everything changes.'

FIVE

The evening was a little chilly, and the Doctor had his coat on. He'd still not had a chance to recover his possessions, and felt almost naked wandering around with empty pockets. He couldn't remember the last time he'd done it. Hundreds of years ago, at the very least. It was also odd not having to plan the rescue of any friends from imminent danger.

Not that he was short of company. Unfortunately. Qerl – the Doctor thought that was his name – was doggedly at his side.

Qerl was a farmer. Dela had left the Doctor with Qerl about two hours ago. It was teatime, and then it was going to be bedtime for the young children. So the Doctor had been stuck with Qerl who, unlike Dela, wasn't terribly prepossessing. They'd spent the whole time discussing soil yields and crop rotation. Qerl was now onto the subject of nitrogen fixation and the Doctor had concluded he would have had a more rewarding chat with a diazotroph.

The Doctor glanced up at the sky. It was evening, so it had gone a very dark green. He couldn't tell where the missing stars would have been. He hadn't spent all that much time in Galaxy Seven, so wasn't familiar with the night sky, and it was clouding over anyway. Peering up, though, he could swear three of the stars were moving in close formation. Before he could confirm it, they were behind a cloud.

Frustrated, the Doctor returned his attention to terrestrial concerns. He'd soon be out of here and heading over to the Fortress. He hoped he could get there before it started raining.

The Council met in the largest tent, which was long and narrow, like an Anglo-Saxon mead hall, and set a little apart from the rest of the settlement, on a raised bit of parkland. The Doctor was welcomed inside. There were ten adults in there, all sitting at one end of rows of short benches. Alsa lounged precociously among them, looking at home. Gar was there, but a wallflower. The adults were dressed in a variety of styles – mostly wraps and robes and saris, that kind of thing – all the clothes were clearly handmade and practical.

Qerl was taking his place on the benches. Jennver stood for a moment, addressing the Doctor rather formally.

'We're here to welcome the Doctor to New Arcopolis.'

A round of polite applause. Jennver took her seat. The Doctor did a little bow, thanked everyone.

'He has already met a great many of us,' Jennver continued. 'It's clear he will fit into this community. He's a very talented individual, and starting to understand how and why we do things here. I suggest we leave it a few weeks until I formally revise the schedule, so we can see which of his many—'

The Doctor had raised his hand.

'Doctor?'

'Er... no,' he said.

Jennver looked puzzled.

'I'm not here for weeks,' the Doctor said.

'But you said you'd help us.'

'Well, yes. For a bit. I did that. I thought you were all gathering this evening to wish me bon voyage.'

Murmuring from the adults.

'Hang on,' the Doctor complained. 'I told you. I was happy to see how I can help out around here. If you'd let me have my sonic screwdriver back, I could have done more, but as it is I've improved the range of the comm mast, given Qerl advice about his berries, serviced—'

'You've done marvellous work,' Jeffip said. 'Don't you like it here?'

'It's lovely,' the Doctor said, aware there was a dash of tetchiness in his voice but unable to remove it. 'Charming. Friendly. But I came to this planet for a reason. There is a weapon inside the Fortress that is very dangerous. I intend to decommission it.'

'I say we let him,' Alsa announced.

Jennver held up a hand, and Alsa fell silent, albeit with bad grace.

'Forgive her, Doctor. As the saying goes: children must find their own way to New Arcopolis.'

'Um... nothing to forgive. I, er, agree with her.' He

looked over at Alsa suspiciously, but the girl was smiling and nodding sweetly.

'You can't go anywhere near the Fortress,' Jennver said. 'If you go there, you will die. There are the ghosts, but there's also the lightning.'

The Doctor decided to be gentle. 'I appreciate that you have a strong taboo against approaching the Fortress. Very sensible. As Alsa will have told you, it's well defended. I have the ability to thwart those defences. I don't mean to boast, but I'm uniquely qualified to do that.'

'You were knocked out by a 13-year-old girl,' Fladon pointed out, to some laughter from the others.

The Doctor could take a joke. 'Indeed. A girl whose life I'd just saved. Perhaps she left that bit out.'

'I told them,' Alsa said, not rising to the bait. 'I've told them everything. We were really close to the Fortress. I think you can do it.'

'Thank you,' the Doctor said, a little unsettled by her magnanimity. 'Now, there will be no danger to anyone here. In fact, after I've deactivated the Fortress, it will be just another building, and you'll be safe to go back into the city.' He smiled at them, tried to keep it cheerful.

'I say we let him,' Alsa repeated.

The Doctor turned to face her, ignoring the others. 'Alsa, with the best will in the world, if you wanted to let me get into the Fortress, why did you hit me with that rock? If you hadn't, I'd have finished the job by now.'

The adults were murmuring again, glancing at him, talking among themselves. Was this the sort of seemingly polite social situation which would abruptly turn into a trial and end with him being thrown down into a pit filled with local carnivores? He'd been the guest of honour at plenty such events, over the years. Come to think of it, there weren't any local carnivores left, were there? So he could relax. Presumably.

The Doctor looked over to Jeffip for some help.

The old man took the hint and stood, bit his lip a little nervously.

'So... Doctor. What would you do after that?'

'Once I've decommissioned the weapon, I'll be on my way. Things will change here, obviously, but it's not up to me to say how.'

Some of the adults were agitated, some angry. No one seemed terribly happy. Except Alsa.

This is why I should avoid politics, the Doctor mused.

'Why abandon us?' Qerl said.

'I'm not "abandoning" anyone. You were getting on fine without me.'

'The problems we have to overcome can't be solved in one day. Another pair of hands, another brilliant mind, could be of such benefit.'

'I know that. I—'

'Why can't you return to us after you've destroyed the weapon?' Jennver suggested.

The Doctor toyed with agreeing. He'd told them the truth before, though, and didn't want to start lying now.

'You don't see the bigger picture,' the Doctor insisted.

Uproar.

'We don't matter?'

The Doctor faltered. 'You matter.'

'But not as much?'

The Doctor's smiled flickered. 'It's not the way I would put it…'

He was saved from being glared to death by Alsa, of all people.

'Look… shut up, everyone. The Doctor's right. There's a bigger picture.'

The Doctor didn't have to wait long for the sting in the tail.

'It's not about him helping out with the crops and chores. Don't you get it? We need the Doctor to do something none of us can: sort out the Fortress. But after that, it doesn't matter if he stays. If he gets rid of the lightning and the ghosts, we can move back into the city.'

Stern silence from the adults, all their attention on the girl.

'Here we go,' moaned Alsa, gearing up for a blazing row. 'Look, we've had good reason to be scared. But it's just a building, there's no magic.'

Jennver sighed. 'We should stay out of the city. All of us.'

'Whyyyyy?'

The members of the Council were shifting in their seats, but had begun to look more relaxed. There's a point in every argument where one of the people crosses the line: goes too far, says something that's demonstrably wrong, steers themselves onto a different point, one that can be knocked down more easily. They all thought Alsa had arrived there.

Jennver was looking kindly at her. 'Because that is

the past and we have to live in the future. We can't be dependent. We need to start afresh, not… cannibalise what was lost. That would be slow suicide.'

'There is a whole city there, full of stuff.'

'A finite amount of "stuff".'

'Plenty for three hundred people. There are apartments with real beds and bathtubs. Tools and other equipment. Games. Clothes. There's just about everything we need and it's going to waste.'

'Once, yes, we could live in the city. Not any more. It isn't practical.'

'Why not?' said Alsa, a real flash of fire in her eyes.

'You wouldn't understand.'

'Oh, here we go. I wasn't alive before. I don't know what it was like before. Life was so different before. I wasn't even born. I know that. I know what it's like now. And it's rubbish. You're scared. That's all it is. Cities are for living in. Let's live in the city.'

It was clear to the Doctor that this was not the first time they'd had this out. The arguments must have been endlessly rehearsed and repeated, and the whole discussion had the air of a well-worn ritual.

Maybe it was his headache, or he wasn't concentrating, but the Doctor couldn't see where Alsa was heading with this, why she thought she'd change anyone's mind this time. Was she just arguing for argument's sake?

'It's not just the ghosts and lightning,' Jennver sighed. 'We can't just move into the ruins.'

The Doctor tried to race ahead of what was being said, tried to get to where Alsa was going. This wasn't just a teenager kicking against the system. Alsa was cunning – the bruise on his head throbbed its agreement at that – and had something up that designer-suited sleeve of hers. What had changed?

Jennver was carrying on with what sounded like a familiar lecture. 'A great city needs lighting, heating. A whole infrastructure, all mechanised. Clean water didn't just miraculously come out the taps, the buildings didn't repair themselves. That was done by machines… and machines need power. We have no way of activating the energy satellites. Unless you have some magical power supply—'

'No!' the Doctor – who had just worked out what Alsa was up to – shouted. 'No. Alsa, no.'

Jennver was distracted, but soon got back to her script. 'Without a power supply for the whole city… we can't live there. We don't even know that the satellites are still there. Jeffip wasted years trying to turn on a small portion of the grid. It wasn't built that way, couldn't be altered. Arcopolis long ago exhausted its fossil fuels. Wood burning just isn't efficient enough.'

The Doctor was on his feet, seriously considering just making a dash for the door. 'The weapon at the heart of that Fortress has to be destroyed.'

Jennver was looking around, bewildered, like he had just changed the subject.

Alsa spelled it out. 'The Fortress. The Doctor says there's this weapon, yeah? He says that it can project holograms and fire death rays, and that there are—'

'We've always known—'

'Yes. We've always known that that thing had a power source. The difference now is the Doctor. He says the Fortress has got infinite power.'

Jeffip had been thinking. 'You know how it runs, Doctor?'

'Yes. The Fortress doesn't have a power plant that also supplies the weapon, it's the other way round: the weapon powers the Fortress. The fact that the Fortress has power is the proof that the weapon is still in there and is still active.'

Alsa smirked. 'Infinite power sounds like plenty to run a city with. That's what the Doctor should be doing: instead of destroying the weapon, he should take that power and harness it.' She pointed straight at him. 'The Doctor can lead us out of the darkness and back where we deserve to be: into a city of light and heat and safety. The Doctor could do that. Don't you see – he's our saviour. Him.'

Everyone was looking straight at the Doctor. Alsa was practically licking her lips, a glint in her eyes.

'If he wants to leave us after that, let him.'

The Doctor closed his eyes, slumped.

'No,' he said.

'If we could harness that power...' Jeffip began.

Fladon was scratching his hairy chin. 'Alsa's right, isn't she, Doctor? You could do this.' It was the first time the Doctor had seen him smile. 'As soon as we get the power back on, we could get some robots running, they'd start fixing things.'

Jennver was looking upset. 'We make our own salvation,' she said in a faltering voice. Then, stronger, 'We will survive through the efforts of our own hands. Not by praying for angels to come down and save us.'

'We don't need to pray, we can just ask,' said Alsa. 'You'll save us, won't you, Doctor?'

He realised he was glaring at her through narrowed eyes.

'No,' he repeated.

Utter silence.

'Can't or won't?' Alsa asked after a moment, leading. She'd known that he would refuse. 'Instead of being selfish and destroying that power source, you connect it up to the grid for us. We can go and live in the city. We could live in the Fortress itself.'

It all sounded so reasonable, but she was so angry. It was infectious, too – the Doctor could feel himself losing his temper.

'I came here to deactivate the Fortress,' he spat. 'Destroy it. Not to do it up as flats.'

'Now you know we're here, though, that changes things, surely?'

'Not enough,' the Doctor said curtly. 'That weapon can't fall into the wrong hands.'

'No space travellers have ever come here. Except you.'

'If they did, having a weapon to defend ourselves wouldn't be a bad idea.'

The Doctor walked up to Fladon, who'd said that, and jabbed a finger at him, before turning to address the other Council members. 'You all saw that? That's how it happens. It starts with "we could really use this around the house" and then – not one minute later – suddenly it's "we could use it to kill our enemies". That's fine when it's a stone tool, or fire, or a knife, or a hunting rifle. It's even fine when it's a missile.' The Doctor hesitated. 'Pushing it a little by that point, admittedly, but it's still fine. The weapon in that Fortress is too powerful.'

Alsa was angry. 'Says who? Too powerful for you, perhaps. Not for us.'

'Doctor, Arcopolis was a place of peace. We had not known war or even serious crime for many thousands of years,' Jeffip said. 'A weapon is no temptation for us.'

'Perhaps the Doctor wants it for himself. We should take stewardship. We know we wouldn't use it.'

'We have no ambitions except survival. We could be guardians of the weapon.'

The Doctor took a deep breath, understood that his answer had to be diplomatic, had to be considered, couldn't under any circumstances include the phrase "you imbeciles". He looked over at Jennver. The leader of the Council hadn't spoken, or even moved, for ages. Her little world was collapsing. She glanced up at him, willed him to say something to convince the others.

'Doctor, we have already experienced the very worst thing that could happen,' Qerl said.

This time, the Doctor couldn't keep it in. 'You think that the worst thing that can possibly happen has already happened, because you've seen one civilisation fall?'

'As the victims of a terrible attack,' Jeffip began, 'I think we can understand the dangers. If the weapon was in our custody, we would prevent it from falling into the hands of people who would misuse it.'

'We lost everything,' Qerl said.

'You don't know the meaning of the word,' the Doctor muttered.

'And the people who built it?' Jeffip asked. 'Won't they just build other weapons like it anyway? They might attack us again.'

'They are all dead,' the Doctor snapped back, 'and there's a lot less of their planet left than there is of this one. The war it was built to fight is long over. That is the last weapon of its type.'

Jennver was looking over at Alsa, thoughtfully. Everyone had lapsed into silence.

The Doctor was beckoning to Jeffip. 'Stand up. Come on. Remind me: what was that you said about star maps?'

'That there was an atmospheric effect that was blocking out the stars, that—'

'The stars were vanishing?'

'Surely you're not suggesting that the weapon's disintegrating stars, one at a time?'

'No.' The Doctor straightened. These were reasonable people. He would reason with them.

'Words like "infinite" and "ultimate"… they're too big. There's an old saying: "One death is a tragedy, a million deaths is a statistic." When you think about the people that died here, I imagine you don't think of the 200 million… you think of your parents, your children, your best friend, even your pets. You remember the countless millions through the ones you cared for.'

He saw a few of them nodding warily, and decided to press his advantage.

'I'll try to explain what this weapon does. All right… imagine you really wanted to destroy your enemy. Really wipe out all trace of them.'

'We don't have enemies, we don't want to destroy anyone.'

'Which is why I said "imagine",' the Doctor said testily. 'Back in the day… the Bronze Age, say, you'd start by burning down your enemy's village if you really wanted to destroy them, not just defeat them or enslave them or steal their stuff—'

'You'd just kill everyone,' interrupted Alsa.

'Exactly. Put them to the sword. Well, put the sword to them, it's far easier. I digress. So… kill all the people. Not just the soldiers, but all the women and children.'

'Barbaric,' Jennver muttered.

'Well, yes. Trouble is: what if someone managed to hide? What if a group of soldiers was out on patrol? What if there was a merchant away from town at the time? Let one puny little boy go and he'll end up as Conan the Barbarian. It's practically the rules. He'll be back.'

'You'd need good information,' Jeffip said.

'Exactly. Know your enemy. But even if you really managed to kill every last person and burn all their stuff, there would be traces. Statues and gravestones. Even bits of broken crockery. You could just about get rid of all that, if you put a lot of effort into it.'

'You wouldn't need to go that far,' Jeffip objected.

'Not normally, no. But what if you did want to remove all traces?'

'You could never remove them all,' Jeffip said.

'Course you could,' Alsa countered. 'If you wanted to hard enough.'

'Even if you dropped a bomb on it you'd leave a crater.'

'And rubble,' the Doctor chipped in. 'Don't underestimate rubble. Even when the last building of Arcopolis falls, there will still be debris. A good archaeologist could come along in 10,000 years and piece things together. After that... well, it's terrible to admit it, but plastics and radioactives and refined metals... pollution, I guess... would be there. You've carved out tunnels and cuttings for roads and so on. But I guess you could build a bomb powerful enough to smash all that to dust. Would that be enough?'

'No,' Alsa said finally.

'No?'

'Because the next village along, they'd remember the destroyed village. They'd be able to... I dunno, draw pictures of it. It would be on their maps.'

The Doctor nodded. 'Good.'

'So you'd have to kill them too,' Alsa added, sounding almost gleeful. 'And... the next village along. And... the...'

Jeffip was thinking it through, now. 'A technological civilisation... one with radio and satellites, you'd have to kill everyone else on the planet. No... more than that, you'd have to go to other planets to make sure they hadn't seen it through telescopes or heard any of their broadcasts. Everything in the light cone.'

'Yes.'

'So... that's what that weapon does?'

The Doctor almost laughed. 'No. That's just if your

enemy lived in one village on one planet. That weapon was designed to use against an enemy with footholds in different galaxies.'

'That would be... impossible.'

'Why?'

'It would be too much work. It would take billions of people thousands of years to do all that.'

'So you build a labour-saving device,' the Doctor said.

Every single person in the room turned to look over his left shoulder. That was the direction of the Fortress.

The Doctor nodded. 'Touch a button and no more enemy. No more traces of enemy. They'd be gone. The weapon doesn't just kill them, it kills everyone who's ever heard of them. Destroys everything they've ever built and drawn and written. Everything they've ever seen, even the stars in their sky. Erases it all. It's a weapon that would give your run-of-the-mill ultimate weapon an inferiority complex.'

'How?' Jeffip asked. 'I mean, how could anything do that?'

The Doctor waved his hand airily. 'Quantum physics. The observer effect. The superforce. Vunktotechnology. Vundatechnology. The people who built that weapon knew their stuff.'

The Doctor checked his watch.

'Wait,' Alsa said. 'Even when it had killed your enemy... there would still be you. You'd be left. You've heard of the enemy. If you wanted to erase every trace, you'd have to kill yourself.'

The Doctor nodded. 'Logically, pretty much whoever

your enemy is, you'd end up destroying the entire universe, including – obviously – yourself. It was a weapon of last resort, to be used only when all was lost.'

'Who would be stupid enough to build a weapon that did that?'

'Building it isn't the issue,' Fladon said.

'No?' the Doctor asked.

'They could build as many as they wanted to. The problem's when you use it.'

The Doctor sighed. '"When" being the operative word.'

'Quite a deterrent,' Jeffip said.

'A what?' Alsa said.

'A threat,' the Doctor said. 'If your opponent knows he's going to be utterly destroyed, he won't attack… four times out of five.'

'I'd attack,' said Alsa.

The Doctor motioned for her to continue.

'Well, if I knew my enemy would destroy themselves when they fired, I'd know they'd never actually fire it. When it came to it, they'd hesitate and –' she mimed herself smashing them.

'When it came to it, they didn't hesitate,' the Doctor pointed out.

'Why is the universe still here?' Alsa asked, sounding almost disappointed. 'What stopped it?'

The Doctor paused.

'I don't know,' he admitted. 'I've asked myself the same question. There might be some kind of protective field around the weapon. If you're near enough, you're immune. It would explain why you survived.'

There was a murmur around the room.

'That travel tube you were all in must have been directly underneath the Fortress when the weapon fired. You must have been within that protective field. Thank heavens for public transport, eh?'

'What happened, Doctor?' Jeffip asked.

The Doctor looked down at his feet. 'They called it an assault, but it wasn't, it was a massacre. Unprovoked, avoidable. And the historians who called it the Last Battle of the Seventh Galaxy didn't even notice Arcopolis. The millions who died here barely qualify as a fraction of the casualty figure.'

'Not even an ant run over by a tank,' Jeffip said weakly. 'Not even a flea on the back of that ant.'

'The weapon in that Fortress has to be destroyed before it can be fired again, and I'm the only person in the entire universe who can destroy it. Now, if you'll excuse me, that's what I'm going to do.'

He turned and strode from the room, hoping against hope no one would try to stop him. Not because he was worried that any of them could, but because he was worried about what he would do to anyone who tried.

SIX

The Doctor's words settled over the room. Out of all the parents, only Jeffip had really reacted. He was staring at the ceiling, like he could see through the plastic sheets and up at the stars. Jennver was quiet and pale.

'Come on, then,' Alsa urged. She was already on her feet.

Fladon was frowning. 'We should only be concerned about the here and now. The children.'

'Agreed,' Qerl called.

'Yeah, yeah: it's all about me,' Alsa said impatiently. 'What are you agreeing to? You're agreeing that we're going to force the Doctor to power up the city. Yes?'

Jeffip didn't understand why Jennver hadn't restored order. 'Did you not hear what he said?'

'What's done is done,' Fladon repeated, to nods of agreement.

'Light years,' Jeffip said. 'Don't you understand? I…'

'The Doctor's getting away,' Alsa complained.

'We know where he's going,' said Jeffip sourly.

Fladon was standing. 'We need to stop him.'

'Look… if we're going to do this—' Jeffip began.

'This?' Alsa said. 'What?'

Jeffip sighed. 'Jennver?'

Jennver looked up. 'The Doctor has ruined everything.'

'I will follow the will of the Council,' Jeffip told her. For so long, that had meant agreeing with its leader. They'd survived. Jennver had delivered every child, organised it all so that each of them had food and shelter.

'We must do what we must,' she whispered.

Fladon took that as an order. 'All right. First of all, let the Doctor get into the Fortress. Alsa, follow him.'

'Ask me nicely.'

'Young lady.'

'I just want you to remember: I saw him first. I brought him here. I showed you what to do next. Showed you things could change. Most of all, I want you to look at Jennver there, and remember that look on her broken old face.' Alsa didn't wait for a response; she was already pulling Gar along.

Jennver looked around. 'Alsa's question was a good one. What exactly are we trying to do? We know what the Doctor wants. Are we really going to force him to do something else?'

Jeffip looked annoyed now. 'We've all been forced to do things we don't like. Why should the Doctor be any different?'

The Doctor met Dela. She was strolling towards him, a

shawl made of foil draped over her shoulders. Her face lit up.

'I was on my way to the Council meeting,' she called out to him as they came closer.

'Go back to your children, Dela.'

She stopped, taken aback.

The Doctor stopped, too. 'I didn't mean it like that.'

The shawl was silver, but with a painted pattern, a sort of abstract leaf design. She'd told him earlier that she painted. They'd talked a lot that afternoon. The shawl was pretty.

'You're angry.'

'Not with you.' The Doctor started walking again. Dela followed. It was a cool evening, the air was moist. It was going to rain.

'You're leaving?'

'Yes.'

'Take me with you.'

'What?'

'You could.'

'No. It's far too dangerous.'

'Not just to the Fortress. To outer space. I don't like it here. I can't defend it the way Jennver and Fladon can. I want to travel with you. In the TARDIS. Be like... Rose.'

The Doctor stopped. They really had talked a lot.

'No.'

'Someone will look after my...' But her voice trailed away. She knew it wasn't that easy.

They'd crossed the threshold into Jeffip's tent. The Doctor took a moment to remember the way to the laboratory.

'New Arcopolis is borderline viable,' he said. 'If I take just one person away from it, there's a chance that everyone else dies. Not only your children. Everyone. You can't leave. You can't.'

She knew that already, of course. 'That's it then? Because of something that happened years ago, something too big to comprehend, there are no choices? Just a treadmill of duties and obligations and no chance of escape?'

'Yes,' the Doctor said. For both of us.

He'd gone the wrong way. This room had a small metal bed and various toolboxes. There was something lying on the bed, covered with a sheet made of the same silvery material as Dela's shawl.

He listened out for a moment, but he didn't think anyone was following them. The Council must still have been arguing about a course of action. He had a few minutes, then.

The Doctor peeked. It was the slender corpse of a teenage girl, in sporty white shorts and camisole top. There was a grey flannel over her face.

'Jall?' he asked.

Dela nodded. 'She was killed by ghosts.'

The Doctor frowned.

'That's been bothering me,' he announced.

'It happens,' said Dela, her voice faltering.

'Are you all right?' the Doctor said.

Dela wasn't. 'She was my daughter. My first child. It happens. If she hadn't been in the city, the ghosts wouldn't have got her. She'd come back, but still visited the city.'

The Doctor shook his head. 'I saw a ghost kill that boy,

er, Frad. He was disintegrated. At the very least. There wasn't a body.'

'You're... right. There's never a body.'

'Oh, I know I'm right. What's that flannel for, do you think?'

Without waiting for a response, the Doctor peeled the flannel off. Dela gasped and stepped back.

Jall's eyes were missing. The Doctor bent over – he'd put his glasses on – and peered into the sockets, with an enthusiasm which was enough to make Dela cough a mild expletive.

'They've only removed the eyeball. Everything else is in there. I mean everything. The bones of the orbit, the optic nerve, the muscles...'

'She had green eyes,' Dela said quietly. 'Really bright green. We joked about who the father was, no one else here has them. Pretty eyes.'

'They wouldn't be so pretty out of context,' the Doctor noted absent-mindedly. 'Sorry, that probably came out a bit horrid, didn't it?'

Dela nodded, swallowed what she had been about to say to him.

'I have no idea how you'd do that.'

'Or why?' she added softly.

The Doctor thought for a moment. 'I'm still stuck on how, I'm afraid,' he admitted. 'There aren't even scratches or bruises on the eyelids. The eyes might have been dissolved, I suppose. Acid. They didn't spill a drop.'

'They?'

'Well, just about the only thing I know for certain is that

this didn't happen spontaneously. And it's just too precise to be an accident. It's... well, I was going to say "surgical", but I don't know any surgeons who could do that good a job. This was a conscious act. The other thing... you don't die if you lose your eyes. So she was killed some other way. No marks on the body, no sign of a struggle. I'd need longer with the body. Hmmm. Did she smoke?'

He placed the flannel back over Jall's face.

'I'm sorry... I don't know what you mean.'

'Cigarettes? Cigar? Pipe? Um... inhale the fumes from dried leaves?'

'We... I don't think anyone in Arcopolis ever did that. Why would you want to? It must be an outer-space thing.'

'It smells like she smoked.'

'I smell it too, now. Perhaps it was something they used to preserve the body.'

The Doctor beamed. 'That makes sense! Well done.'

'Thanks.'

'It wasn't something they used to preserve the body.'

He put the foil sheet back and swept from the room. Dela hurried after him, after a glance back at the shape under the silver foil.

Dela showed him the way to Jeffip's laboratory.

The Doctor removed the sonic screwdriver from the vice and clipped the casing back together. He slipped it into his pocket and did the same with the psychic paper, the ball of string, the anti-radiation pills, the pocket Gallifreyan-Cymraeg phrasebook, the bag of kola nuts, the yo-yo, a collection of coins from a dozen different planets, the everlasting matches, the TARDIS key and everything else of his.

'Come back,' Dela told him. Her eyes were wet, she was still thinking about her daughter.

The Doctor put his hand on her shoulder. 'I will. I'll find out who did that to Jall.'

'And punish them for it?'

The Doctor's eyes flashed fire. 'Oh yes.'

It was a warm night, and it was beginning to rain.

The Doctor had been unconscious when he'd been brought here, but he'd spent the day since looking out to the Fortress, memorising the landmarks of the Arcopolis skyline. He had his escape route worked out. There were no walls or fences – why would there be? – but the river blocked off the most direct route to the Fortress.

He followed the course of the river, heading past the mill upstream. He was away from the tents in minutes, moving quickly until he was out of the park and into the city. It was raining heavily by then, so he confined his route to covered walkways, or at least routes that had some form of shelter.

The city was noisy, with all the rainwater glugging and surging through drains and sewers and pipes. When Arcopolis had been inhabited, the gutters and pumps would have been maintained. Now, they were rusted shut or worn away or plugged up. The city and the rainfall would wrestle with each other, trying to get the other to give way. There would be different results in different parts of the city.

It was dark. It would make him difficult to spot, but would give anyone following him the same advantage. They knew he was heading for the Fortress, so they didn't need to pursue him, just show up there. He still didn't have a canoe, so he'd approach the Fortress from the opposite side, perhaps try one of the half-buildings. It would take him until morning to get there, and then he'd use the sunlight to assess the best way in.

The Doctor passed a white dome that must have once gleamed. Now it was grubby, cracked open like a boiled egg. Half a dozen boys in colourful suits of armour they'd improvised from sports equipment and padding huddled in there, against the rain and the cold. They might even have seen him, but apparently he wasn't worth getting drenched for.

Above them all, a clear plastic walkway was sloshing with water, like a log flume. The ground was very soft. There was a crack of thunder. This wasn't anything more than a simple storm, but the buildings that surrounded him were fragile things, and the water could easily dislodge a piece of masonry or plate glass and send it hurtling down at him.

Midnight, or near enough, and the Doctor was picking his way over a broken slope of tiles. Moss had squeezed out through the gaps, cracked the ceramic. This had been a wide plaza. The tiles were white, and, even at night, the contrast of the tiles and the growth between made for a vivid, just-about-regular grid pattern. In the middle of the plaza was a great circular shape. It had once been a fountain, but it had collapsed in on itself, cracked, filled up to overflowing with giant lilies.

The rain had eased up, but the ground was still slick and the air cool and damp. It smelled sharp, earthy, rusty. A little like blood, the Doctor thought.

A glass man was no more than a dozen paces ahead of him, facing to the Doctor's right. It was an abstract human figure, almost featureless. It was the size of a small adult and slightly pot-bellied, or at least it had very poor posture. It didn't move as he approached.

Whatever it was, it wasn't a ghost. The Doctor concluded that it was a statue, after all.

The glass man turned its head, took a step back, as though it was only now aware of the Doctor and had been startled by his presence. The face was almost smooth, with tiny bumps and crevices instead of a nose and mouth.

It was too dark to make out much detail, all the Doctor could see was how the figure distorted the scene behind it, so the Doctor took another step forward. The glass man raised a six-fingered hand, in what would have been a defensive gesture if a human being – or Time Lord, for that matter – had made it. There was a golden disc set into the palm of the creature's hand.

'I'm not trying to hurt you. I'm the Doctor, by the way.'

It lowered the arm, then started to run, an almost comical sight as it barely moved its arms or upper body, just its legs.

The Doctor gave chase, but the glass man could clearly outrun him. For one thing, despite having bare, glass feet, it had a better grip on the slick tiles than the Doctor's trainers could manage. He discovered that as they turned a sharp corner. For another, the Doctor had spent all night picking over wet and uneven ground and was beginning to ache from the exertion. It didn't stop the Doctor trying, but he soon fell behind.

The glass man ran through an open doorway into a deserted building, and by the time the Doctor caught up to that, he couldn't hear its thumping, solid footsteps any more. It had got away.

The Doctor was a little out of breath.

Someone was standing over Alsa. Before she was fully awake, she'd lashed out at him.

Gar managed to dodge her hand. 'It's me,' he hissed.

All around them, children were stirring. It was getting light.

'They've spotted him heading into the Car Factory.'

Alsa nodded. It was starting to come back to her.

Last night, she'd used the comm to contact two dozen boys and a couple of girls, not always the strongest or tallest, but the toughest. Most of them were already within a few hours of the Fortress, and most would drag other kids there with them. Alsa had spent a quarter of an hour in the settlement stuffing things into bags and pulling together rainwear before heading off with Gar.

She'd met a few others at the Tesla Farm, a field of giant ceramic cones close to the settlement, where the kids had built up a good stash: torches, binoculars, energy drinks and loads of other stuff the parents disapproved of. One of the things they hated most was bicycles. Alsa never understood that. You could race around on bikes, and they were simple enough to fix – only the chains were even a little bit complicated. The tyres got punctured, yeah, but they could be patched. Alsa, obviously, didn't bother; she just found a spare on some bike rack or shop. Usually, she'd just ditch the whole original bike.

She smirked when she thought of the Council actually giving her permission to go to the Fortress – although she'd been the one giving the orders. It had taken two hours by bike, so she, Gar and the others had shown up there around eleven and taken position.

By then, just about everyone she'd commed was there, and they'd posted watch on all the approaches. She had taken the plum position, in an old clock tower, right in the middle of the Car Factory. She'd worn herself out doing all that, and was soon asleep.

'Any ghosts?'

'Vrem said he'd seen one, but he's a liar.'

Alsa shoved Gar out of the way of the window.

The Car Factory was a simple building – a 115-storey white concrete doughnut with sweeping windows and gaping hangar doors dotted irregularly at every level. The Fortress had materialised so that one of its black walls had just taken a bite out of the doughnut. From her vantage point, right in the hole of the doughnut, Alsa could look down on the entire complex, even into a lot of the Factory building. There was a metal skywalk that gently spiralled down from the top of the clock tower to the roof of the Car Factory, and then down to ground level. Cycling down that was going to make the effort of pushing the bikes up worth it. The Factory covered such a wide area that they were well out of range of the lightning here but, in the past, plenty of kids had strayed from a safe level and had never been seen or heard of again. Her various lookouts were all well outside that perimeter.

The parents never told them anything about Arcopolis or the old days, but sometimes they'd let slip something, or an adult would set a child straight. To Alsa, aircars had always been lumps of metal, prone to toppling over if you played too hard or got too frisky in them. She'd never found it that easy to picture them soaring over and swooping between the buildings. Alsa had sat in plenty of aircar seats, been surprised how comfortable they were, how many controls and lights and switches there were. Robots and computers used to stop them from crashing – Alsa was unclear exactly how.

She knew some of the number symbols, and if she was reading them right these cars could fly 300 miles a day. They could have travelled from the settlement to the Fortress in minutes, not hours, and carried loads of stuff. You wouldn't be tired or wet when you got there, either.

If the Doctor was from space, why didn't he bring an aircar? She'd ask him when she caught up with him.

She spotted the Doctor walking under a twenty-storey sign. The sign was made up of bright glass tubes. Some of the kids said that they heard that in the olden days signs like that used to light up at night because there was a special gas in them, but Alsa didn't believe in that. The sign was amazing enough as it was.

The Doctor looked tired, but not exhausted. That odd

brown coat of his was darker because it was so wet. His stupid spiky hair had gone flat and stuck to his scalp. She'd guessed the Doctor would come this way. He knew there was an impassable lake on the other side of the Fortress, and the other ways in had open plazas which would be just as deadly. The Car Factory was one of the half-buildings he'd been so fascinated by, and the one that was the biggest and best landmark.

'What's the plan?' Gar asked.

'We comm the parents. Let them know we've seen the Doctor. Tell them we'll wait for them to get here.' The way Alsa smiled made Gar feel very nervous.

SEVEN

The doughnut-shaped factory building was vast. Over a hundred identical floors, each with a high ceiling and its own production line, all stacked on top of each other. Each line ended with its own massive door, just waiting for the finished aircars to fly out of it. The production process had been, as far as the Doctor could tell, entirely automated. Sunlight streamed through great, wide windows. There were a few gantries and inspection ladders for people, and the Doctor used them where he could, but mainly he just walked along the conveyor belts. The floors were covered in dried-up pools of paints, glues and other liquids which must have escaped from pipes and cans over the years, when their seals had failed. It brought splashes of colour and unpredictability to a sterile white and chrome environment.

The production line, robot workers and all, had frozen in place fifteen years ago. It meant that the Doctor was now a fascinated visitor to a museum featuring tableaux of a state-of-the-art Arcopolis factory. For half an hour, he almost forgot about the Fortress, the villagers who'd be on his trail, Dela and Jall, the ghosts, the glass man and everything else. He put on his glasses to get a closer look at a few things, he tapped and prodded and danced around. He'd found a device that was basically a sonic screwdriver but was the size and shape of a car wash. Jeffip had mentioned it. He speculated how quickly a car could have been put together. He marvelled how every stage of the process was so flexible that each car was practically custom-built to order. In a city of 200 million people, there probably weren't two aircars the same.

Then he'd followed the great curved path along too far, and found himself faced by the sheer black wall of the Fortress.

He did the traditional, dodging behind a great stack of engine blocks to avoid the blue energy bolt that came hurtling past. A window thirty metres behind him shattered and threw down daggers of glass and strips of concrete window frame.

The Doctor peeked through gaps in the stack. The wall was matt black, at an angle almost exactly forty-five degrees to the factory floor. Mounted on the Fortress wall, he could see the gun turret, a thin wisp of smoke curling up from the barrel.

The gnarled black walls of the Fortress looked almost fused with the smooth white concrete of the Factory. Fifteen years ago, the Fortress would have materialised in the city, like the TARDIS materialised. Unlike the TARDIS, there weren't all sorts of safety systems, and the things it landed on would have been instantly annihilated. It was, while horrible, quite an elegant solution. The universe wasn't designed to have big things like Fortresses suddenly appear from nowhere. The energy created by destroying so much matter was fed back into the transduction corridor, helping to balance the books of cosmic physics.

The Doctor clacked his tongue. He knew what the factory was made of – diamond-reinforced type five space concrete. He didn't know for sure what the Fortress was made of – it was ugly black stuff that was probably metal or something. He wished there was someone here so he could tell him or her just how much of an expert he was on particle transduction and how all this knowledge meant he understood precisely how the Fortress and factory fitted together.

He fiddled with the sonic screwdriver, adjusting a couple of its settings with the deft touch of a safecracker.

'There's a problem with diamond-reinforced type five space concrete…' began the Doctor, talking to no one in particular.

He pointed the sonic screwdriver at the roof and it squealed for a few seconds.

A crack appeared, right above the Doctor's head. The crack spread, then started to speed up. It raced in one direction, towards the outer wall. At the last possible moment, it kinked to the left, hit a point where the ceiling met the Fortress.

A tiny piece of concrete, a pebble, fell, pinged against the Fortress wall, skipped and pinged again. The gun turret swivelled until it was pointing straight up, fired and atomised the pebble. The energy bolt kept going, slammed into the cracked ceiling. The roof shattered, and a large chunk of it dropped onto the gun, bending it in half. A moment later, a cascade of smaller pieces of concrete rained down, flattening the remains of the weapon.

'... and that's that it's easy to resonate.' He looked down at the sonic screwdriver. 'I've never resonated concrete on my own before. That was fun.'

He sauntered over to the Fortress wall, thought about it for a moment, and then slapped it with his hand. It clanged like a bell. Common-or-garden ugly black stuff that was probably metal. He found a seam and opened it up, pulling back a panel that was so thick he needed both hands to hold it. Once he had slid it aside, there was a gap there just wide enough for him to squeeze through. So he did.

The Doctor had entered the Fortress.

Alsa, Gar and a couple of other kids – brothers called Coz and Moz – were running along a rubber and metal pathway that curved along the middle of this level of the Car Factory. It was easier to get around on foot here than on bikes.

'Where is he?' Gar moaned.

'It's not this floor,' Alsa said impatiently, 'it's the next one up.'

They weren't that far from where the Fortress bit into the factory. They would have had to slow down anyway.

There was the sound of shattering glass, from upstairs.

They all dived behind a nearby machine. It was a white thing, it looked like a miniature crane, with a whole set of sharp tools on the tip of its arm. Looking up at it while she caught her breath, Alsa thought it might be a robot arm. The thought of robots that were just bits of people had always disturbed her when she was younger.

There was a crack and the sound of a rockslide.

The four of them were covering their faces instinctively. You got used to the buildings crumbling.

'The floor above,' Coz said.

'The Doctor,' Alsa agreed, not taking her eyes off the ceiling. They had to get to him before he got inside.

'It was falling on metal, not concrete. He's set off a bomb that's blown a hole in the wall of the Fortress.'

'Nah. Whole point of a Fortress is that you can't just slap a bomb on the wall. Anything strong enough to damage the Fortress would have ripped this place apart.'

Gar was confused. 'We have to wait for the parents.'

'It'll take them hours to get here,' Moz complained. 'They told us to wait.'

'Wait?' Coz wailed.

'It took us two or three hours on bikes,' Alsa said. 'And they'll be walking. We let the Doctor open a way into the Fortress. After that, we grab him. It's been the plan all along.'

'Has it? First I've heard,' Gar noted.

'Yeah, well, it wasn't your plan. Can you imagine all the incredible stuff there must be in the Fortress?'

The boys all snickered.

'I can't, and neither can you,' Jeffip said.

All four kids sat bolt upright. Professor Jeffip was there. So were Fladon and Dela. Dela was Coz and Moz's mum.

'How?' Moz said.

'We lived in Arcopolis long before you ever came here, Morren,' Dela said.

'I used to be a supervisor at this factory,' Fladon said, talking to the other adults. 'I was here four years, and they said the robots were foolproof, but once, one of them broke down and...' He hesitated. 'Another robot had to fix it. Sorry, it seemed a lot more dramatic at the time.'

Dela laughed and put her hand on Fladon's shoulder. 'A lot of us worked round here, remember?'

Alsa's blood was boiling. This wasn't where the parents came, this was where the kids came.

'Oh, calm down, Alsa,' Dela said. It was exactly the same tone of voice she used with the babies.

'How did you get here?'

'Think about it. It takes hours to get here from the settlement. We had to get here quickly, not just wait for the call.'

'So you were right behind us last night?'

Jeffip chuckled. 'About an hour behind you, yes. We waited until it stopped raining.'

'If it's any consolation,' Fladon said, 'the walk's just about worn all three of us out.'

Professor Jeffip coughed, leaning on his walking stick as he bent over. Jeffip was ancient. He was pale and out of breath. He'd just walked something like twenty miles, in the wet. Alsa admired the fact he had it in him.

'Are you all right?' she asked.

Fladon looked concerned. 'If anything was to happen to you, Jeffip, the settlement—'

He waved everyone away. 'It's a cough. Come on. Let's get up there.'

Fladon knew a quick way to the next floor, and soon they were up there and edging around. All of them felt uneasy so close to the black wall, even when they saw a pile of rubble where a gun should have been.

No one else saw it, and it was a whole minute before even Alsa saw the tiny gap in the wall. The Doctor must have opened it up. There was no sign of him.

'I don't think I could squeeze through that,' Fladon admitted.

'I could,' Alsa insisted.

'We shouldn't,' Fladon warned. 'It's too risky.'

Alsa was running for the gap.

'Wait!' everyone else was calling. They were chickens. A chicken was an extinct animal that was scared of everything. That's what Jeffip and Dela were like. Fladon and Gar just did what they were told.

Gar was at Alsa's side.

'You coming with me?' she asked.

'No,' he said, trying to block her way.

'Doesn't matter,' she said, pushing him over. She ducked through the slit in the Fortress wall. No one else had the courage to follow her.

It was dark inside the Fortress. Black walls and no windows, the exact opposite of the Car Factory. It took a moment for Alsa's eyes to adjust.

She pushed forwards, found she was in a thin crawlspace

between two layers of wall. She edged along. The roof was angled, making it difficult to stand up. Her heart was racing, the blood rushing around her, scared and angry.

Alsa realised that she was already disorientated.

The ceiling sloped, she realised. The higher side was the inside. Alsa knew roughly how big the Fortress was – the outer wall was about a mile long and at the end of it was just a sharp turn then another mile of wall. What if the crawlspace floor didn't run all that way? It was so dark, she'd just plummet.

'Stay back!' the Doctor's voice hissed, and from about six inches away. 'Stay exactly where you are, or we'll both be killed!'

Outside, everyone was so busy worrying about Alsa and debating whether they should go back or stay where they were that it was at least thirty seconds before any of them noticed the glass man. Jeffip was the first. He didn't say anything, just tapped Dela on the shoulder.

The new arrival was in front of a wide window. With sunlight pouring through its transparent body, it was possible for Dela to see that there were… things inside it. A dozen or so tiny, indistinct shapes.

The humans all just looked around at each other, baffled. No one was sure what they were looking at.

'We need to leave,' Fladon suggested.

'No…' Jeffip said, his voice trailing away.

Then they all heard it, even though it was only in their heads.

'Here.'

'Was he talking to us?' Dela whispered.

Dela was looking past the glass man and out of the window. A structure was pushing down through the green sky. It was bone-white, and looked like a number of flat shapes slotted together. It was difficult to judge the size, but it was immense, as large as a city block, at least. A central disc with three or four long flat pieces at a right angle to it, with smaller triangles and dozens of squares fitted at different angles to those long pieces, a little like sails on the mast of an ancient galleon. There was a glowing golden sphere beneath the disc, just hanging there.

Two others, the same size and shape, were behind it. They were too strange to be entirely beautiful.

'Spacecraft,' Jeffip said. He'd joined Dela. She hadn't even noticed him alongside her until he spoke.

'Is that one of the people that built the Fortress?' Dela asked, indicating the glass man.

'The Doctor said they were all dead. He could be wrong, but… those ships don't look anything like the Fortress.'

'Does a spaceship have to look like a skyscraper?'

Jeffip, of course, had anticipated the question. 'It doesn't look like it shares anything. No materials, no design elements. No… philosophy.'

Jeffip took a step forward, and everyone else tensed up.

'I know what I'm doing,' he told them. 'I have to contact these people. Warn them.'

'I was being careful,' Alsa complained.

The Doctor appeared in a circle of white light. Alsa realised that he'd taken the torch from her bag, which meant it had occurred to him she might have it and taken it before she'd even remembered it was there. 'Good. Not slowly enough, though. Think of this place as a giant unexploded bomb. The slightest wrong move and there's no negotiating or tricks, the machines running this place will kill us.'

'I got past the defences.'

The Doctor laughed, and there was more than a hint of disdain. 'There are thousands of defence systems and they don't stop at the outer wall. They're almost all on standby at the moment.'

'Standby?'

'You know. Like a TV that's on but not really on… ah, I see the problem. You don't watch enough television. You should. Five hours a day, minimum, and sit really close to the screen. OK… what's the best way to explain? Oh… easy. Easy-peasy: this Fortress is asleep. It will wake up if we disturb it.'

'How do you disturb a building? It's just, well, a building isn't it?'

The Doctor shook his head, thought about it, then nodded.

'That's not much help.'

'I don't know the answer to your question. Inside here are loads of detectors. They send data to a battle computer, a sort of machine with a brain—'

'I know what a computer was,' Alsa told him.

'—which works out if there's anything worth bothering with. I don't know precisely how it makes that calculation.'

'So we don't know the rules.'

'The monsters that designed this place didn't tell anyone the rules, because they didn't want anyone winning the game.'

The Doctor swung the torch back the way Alsa had come. 'Right. You've got just as much chance of setting everything off if you go back. So stick with me. Don't do anything unless you've seen me do it, don't step anywhere I haven't stepped, don't touch anything unless I've touched it. No, scratch that: don't touch anything. If you see a rock, don't hit me over the head with it, if you can manage that.'

'No promises.' But the Doctor knew what he was doing, and she needed him around, at least for the moment.

The Doctor handed her back the torch and took out something from his pocket. The same device he'd recharged her comm with. The end lit up, there was a buzzing sound and a hatch on the inner wall popped open.

The Doctor smiled. 'As long as you are the only distraction, we'll be fine. Five times out of five. Well... two times out of... erm... I'm sure we'll be fine. As long as no one does anything stupid.'

Jeffip walked over to the glass man. He paused, probably considering what to say.

It was strange. Dela felt a connection with this creature, like it knew her. She regretted that it wasn't mutual. She wasn't totally convinced it was alive – not even partially, like robots. Through the window, she could see the three alien spaceships. They were miles away but, between them, they filled the air. White against the green sky, they could have been freak, sculpted storm clouds with rays of sunlight peeking out from underneath them. Just about.

'I am Jeffip,' the old man said, so quietly that Dela and the others could barely hear him. 'I am a native of this world. I welcome you to Arcopolis.'

But the glass man walked straight past him. Now it was walking towards Dela. It moved with such grace. The light sparkled off it. Behind it, through the window, the beautiful, pristine spaceships were such a contrast to the dilapidated towers and fallen spires of Arcopolis.

Dela was now shoulder to shoulder with the glass man.

It turned its head. For the first time, she could see its face. Dela was so close she couldn't see anything else.

'We are the Eyeless,' it announced.

'But you...' Dela began.

It had eyes. Just the eyeballs, one above the other, not side-by-side. They looked just like a human being's eyes, just little blobs of white jelly, but they were suspended in the transparent form of its head. With no eyelids or eye sockets, the eyes looked too large, and all they did – all they could do – was stare wildly at her.

The irises were bright green.

She recognised the eyes and so she knew where the glass man had got them.

Dela screamed.

PART TWO
UNLESS

EIGHT

How do you define intelligence? It's a word that means different things to different people. The scientists who built the Fortress weren't worried so much about an abstract debate. They needed a practical answer.

The Fortress could have been given an artificial mind so brilliant, so adaptable, that it would be able to solve any problem instantly by thinking it through. Imagine a student who was brilliant at mathematics, and so was smart enough to pass any maths exam or test. But the idea of creating so powerful a mind worried the builders of the Fortress. They knew plenty of examples of creations rising up and destroying their creators, and they couldn't take the risk. This Fortress would have access to the ultimate weapon, and making it intelligent and resourceful was just asking for trouble. Luckily, there was another way of doing it. Imagine a second student, one who had been given a list of all the answers. He would also get a perfect score. Most people would say that it was only the first student who was really demonstrating 'intelligence', but the results would be identical.

The Fortress had been given a giant list of every possible problem and the best solutions. Its builders had set it up so that the Fortress would automatically perform the required action.

The Fortress 'thought'. It received information from millions of sensors dotted inside and outside the building, but it didn't have a 'brain' as such. There wasn't even one place where it did its thinking – that would have been far too vulnerable to attack – so there were hundreds of tiny computers, all linked up in dozens of different ways. It didn't know right from wrong, any more than a dishwasher knows what a dish is.

The sensors could see, hear, taste, touch and smell things far more efficiently than a human being could. It knew that some forms of attack would be based on deception – that it couldn't always believe its own eyes and ears. So it didn't just check what it was seeing once, it asked itself thousands of times a second.

What it sensed now were a couple of humanoids that had got inside. They posed no immediate threat, and there was an extremely high probability that they would trigger one of the automatic defences.

The best model that matched said that there was no need to intervene and the intruders would soon be dead.

The Doctor hadn't heard the voice.

Alsa was two steps behind him. They were in a narrow corridor which was made – floors, walls and ceiling – of the same black metal as the outside of the Fortress. It soaked up the light, just giving them enough to see their feet and the route ahead.

'It said something about a list. I think,' Alsa told him.

'I didn't hear anything,' the Doctor said. He continued striding on, moving quickly but controlling every single movement, careful where he planted every footstep, every glance.

'"We are a list",' said Alsa.

'"We are a list"?' the Doctor repeated, scoffing.

'The voice was dead faint. Like it was back outside.'

The corridor twisted downhill, and was lit by dull green electric lamps. Alsa was impressed by the clean, even quality of the light. The most impressive thing was that the lights were just... there. Light usually meant keeping an eye out to make sure the poppy oil wasn't running low or the flame wasn't too high, that there was enough ventilation. She had never taken light for granted. There weren't all that many things she'd ever taken for granted.

It was the first place she'd been that felt normal. Not ruined or bound up in a load of stupid rules. The place smelled clean. This wasn't a warm place, but it had solid walls and a dry floor. For all the black metal and darkness, Alsa felt more at home here than she ever had before.

The Doctor wasn't saying very much. There hadn't been any of his grinning or fooling around. He'd turned to look back a couple of times, and the expression on his face was grim.

Alsa wasn't sure what her plan was at this stage. She knew where she wanted to get to; the weapon plugged into the city power grid. She knew not even Professor Jeffip would be able to do that; it would have to be the Doctor. She hadn't worked out, yet, how to force the Doctor to do it. For now, she'd just stick close to him.

He had some idea of the layout of the place. They'd only been walking for a few minutes, but it felt like they were making good progress. The Doctor had already defused a device that he said had been poised to electrocute them. 'Kill us with electricity,' he'd explained cheerfully, as he handed Alsa a piece of mechanism he'd barbecued with the sonic screwdriver.

The corridor broadened out into a small circular room.

'It's safe,' the Doctor said, hesitating just long enough to give away that he was guessing. There were two open doorways leading out of the room. The Doctor was rubbing his lips thoughtfully.

'Hmmmm,' he said. 'Hand your comm over, I've had an idea.'

Alsa scowled at him.

'Please?'

She passed the bag over. The Doctor quickly found the comm. He was thumbing at the controls the moment he had it in his hand and, within seconds, a hologram of the Fortress was flickering above the comm display.

'How did you get it to do that?'

'I hacked into the Fortress battle computer.'

The hologram showed a green and blue wire-frame representation of the outside of the Fortress. The native buildings of Arcopolis were marked out in white lines. Alsa tried to take in as much of it as she could. More and more details started to fill in on the hologram, apparently as a result of the Doctor's playing around. Now it was showing the internal structure, thick layers of walls opening into a large vault. In the centre of the building was a column with its roots in the base and whose trunk reached up to the very apex of the roof.

None of those things were occupying Alsa's attention.

'Do you recognise those?' she asked, indicating three vast objects shown floating outside the Fortress. They were hovering over the far shore of the lake.

'They look a bit like the *Blue Peter* ship,' the Doctor said, distracted. 'They're probably not though,' he added.

Alsa was shaking her head.

'Hang on,' said the Doctor.

One word flashed up on the tiny screen.

EYELESS

'Eyeless?' the Doctor said, puzzled.

'It's the people who built this place,' Alsa said. 'They know we're in here, and they're angry.'

'Definitely not, probably not, and very possibly,' the Doctor said. 'In that order.'

'That voice didn't say "a list", it said "eyeless". What's it mean?'

'That they don't need mascara, monocles or an optician?' The Doctor sniffed, clearly more interested in what the comm was telling him. 'That they're fearless and earless and peerless and tearless?'

'They're aliens,' Alsa said impatiently. 'If they're not the people who built the Fortress, are these the aliens that the Fortress was built to fight?'

'No.'

'So they're a fourth lot?'

'Third, surely…'

'The ones who built the Fortress. The ones they were fighting. You.'

'Ah. Well, yes, then they're a fourth lot.'

'You met this type before? Know what they look like?' Alsa asked.

'Eyeless?' the Doctor said. 'Not from just the name. Eyeless? Eyeless! No. I've only been to Galaxy Seven a handful of times, mind. I'm in a state of Eyelesslessness.'

Alsa looked around for a rock to hit him with, but there wasn't one.

'Do not move,' a voice said. 'Stop what you are doing, Doctor.'

'Doctor,' Alsa warned.

The Doctor sighed. 'Oh, what is it now?'

'You didn't hear that?'

'You hearing the voices again?' He didn't trust her.

'The same voice,' Alsa insisted.

'What did it say?' he asked, not sounding interested.

'"Do not move",' Alsa said.

'A rather stupid thing to say. Unless it was in here with—'

They had been followed in. The Doctor and Alsa turned to see three glass men walking down into the alcove, taking up position to block all the exits.

A few minutes earlier, when she'd first seen the bright green eyes, Dela had been sick, helpless as the glass man stood over her. The eyeballs were just fixed in its head, watching her. How could they even be functional? Was it wearing them as decoration, like she used to wear jewellery?

She had remembered the Doctor's promise to find and punish whoever had done that to Jall.

Jall?

Jall. An image of her: those bright green eyes where they belonged, the two of them laughing. A month before, when Jall had come back and they'd talked all night, and Dela discovered that yet another cliché of motherhood – that your daughter grew to be a friend – could be true.

Dela had looked up to see Jall's dead eyes peering down at her.

The Eyeless had been reading her mind, taking her memories. Dela had tried to resist, but realised she didn't know how to begin fighting it off. It stole another memory, the last one she had of the Doctor, of him running off into the night. Then another, of her arriving on this floor of the Car Factory, seeing the opening in the Fortress wall.

The Eyeless had stayed in her mind but, as it had turned to face the black metal wall, it was as if it had loosened its grip a little, and there was enough slack for Dela to have new thoughts. She had got up, legs shaking, wanting to leave.

Six more Eyeless had marched in, keeping perfect formation. Three at the front, two in the middle, one at the end.

People were allowed secrets. There were things no one else knew about her. All of them had spilled out, the Eyeless lapping them all up, not appreciating their value. Dela had felt the same sense of violation and frustration she'd had when she was fifteen, when she'd seen the settings had changed on her diary and realised her mother had been reading it, and so she knew about Gyll.

Had she just remembered that, or had the Eyeless remembered it for her?

Dela had wanted to slap it. No – break it. It was glass. Surely a blow from a blunt, heavy object could crack it open?

The dead eyes had stared down at her, and Dela had understood that it didn't mean to hurt her. Instead she was a resource, a well of knowledge about the Doctor, so she had value.

'The Doctor is a threat,' it had said, and a wave of agreement had broken inside Dela's head. The Eyeless had turned on its heel, and marched over to the gap in the Fortress wall opened up by the Doctor. Two others had joined it.

'We have an opportunity to study the Doctor. We must enter now.'

And, knowing she couldn't just abandon the Doctor and Alsa, but too scared to go into the Fortress after them, all Dela had found she could do, as she stood there and the minutes had ticked by, was feel sick again.

The Doctor had allowed himself to get distracted. If he'd stuck to his plan, not been knocked out by that girl, then he would have been and gone before the Eyeless showed up. But then, if that had happened, he'd never have met an Eyeless. And now he'd met three.

'Hello there,' he said cheerfully, picking one to talk to. 'I'm the Doctor, by the way. I met you earlier. You ran off.'

The Eyeless were shorter than the Doctor, but towered over Alsa. This one regarded the Doctor silently for a good half a minute.

'You really can't hear it speak, can you?' Alsa asked the Doctor, delighted.

'It doesn't have a mouth,' the Doctor pointed out.

He went over to it. So, this was an Eyeless. This was the first time he'd got the chance for a proper look, so he put on his spectacles.

It looked like glass, but was perhaps clear resin or plastic. It looked hard, but might have been soft, like gel. Or sticky. It was all the Doctor could do to stop himself from poking it.

Whatever it was made of was almost flawless, but there were a few small bubbles in there. Other items, too – things that he didn't understand. In this nearest one, there was what looked like a red cog, about a centimetre in diameter embedded in its leg; a small V-shaped tube of plastic in its neck; a gold disc in its hand; what looked like a seventeen-centimetre strip of stir-fried beef in its chest. None of these objects seemed to be connected to anything, and he couldn't see for the life of him what function they served. Were they decorative? Did they have some ritual purpose? Oh, come on, Doctor – 'some ritual purpose' is what people say when they don't want to admit they haven't a clue what an artefact is.

'Well, look at you,' the Doctor beamed, genuinely thrilled. 'I have to admit, I think you've caught me out. No joints, no muscles, no seams, no capillary tubes. I thought you might be using nanotechnology, but you're not, are you? You're not a robot. A silicon-based life form. Or... oh, wait. Carbon-based, like me and Alsa, but the carbon takes the form of diamonds? Is that it? Are you a diamond geezer? You look completely solid, but you can move. Animated glass. That really is remarkable. Are you going to tell me how it's done, or is it a secret?'

Ten seconds of absolute silence.

'I don't think he can,' Alsa said, then, more petulant, 'I don't know why not. I'm just telling you.'

'Is it talking to you? In your head?'

Alsa nodded.

'Telepaths. A race of glass telepaths called the Eyeless. I mean, cor, how brilliant is that? I can't hear it. Can it hear me?'

'The entire surface of his body can register the smallest vibrations in the air. It's far more sensitive to sound than a human ear.'

The Doctor turned back to his Eyeless, grinning. He opened and closed his mouth for a few seconds, made hand gestures, pretending to speak but with no words coming out.

'No,' said Alsa, a couple of beats after he'd finished. 'I think he's dead clever and just pretending.'

'I am,' the Doctor nodded solemnly. 'But I'm not clever enough to work out why you call yourself "the Eyeless".'

'That's obvious,' Alsa scowled.

'It's obvious they don't have eyes, but why didn't they pick their noses?'

Alsa sniggered, and it was a moment before the Doctor worked out why.

'You know what I mean,' he insisted. 'They don't have noses, either. Why not the Noseless, eh? Or the Mouthless? Hairless? Earless? Heartless?'

'Can't they call themselves whatever they want?' Alsa asked.

The Doctor thought about it for a few seconds more, tried to clarify his objection. 'Groups are usually named after where they come from, or what they do, or what they believe in, or what they want to be. What sort of culture names themselves after something they aren't? Something they don't have? Something that's not theirs?'

The question hung in the air.

'What are they, Alsa?'

'They're trying to explain. I don't understand.'

'Say what you see,' the Doctor suggested.

'There are white things, like… structures, all gathered around a huge ball that looks like the sun, but it's in the middle of the night sky. The structures, there are thousands of them. They're buildings and vehicles, but also parts of a machine. There are loads of Eyelesses in them, all bathed in colourful light. They travel all across the galaxy. It's incredible.'

The Doctor could have worked most of that out for himself.

'Why?' he asked.

The Eyeless didn't say anything, but the question clearly confused them.

'They forage for technology. Because they can read

minds, they usually find it easy to come to an arrangement with the original owners. If not, they take what they want anyway,' Alsa grinned. 'They're just like me.'

The Doctor raised an eyebrow. 'Are they, now?'

Alsa laughed. 'They've just promised to change things here.'

'Have they, indeed?'

'They don't trust you,' Alsa told him. 'They say I shouldn't trust you.'

'They're used to reading minds. They've never needed to earn trust, just taken it. Takers. That's what they are. Scavengers. Thieves. Thugs. On a cosmic scale.'

'They want to know why they can't read your mind.'

The Doctor jabbed his thumb at his chest. 'Time Lord. We come with top-of-the-line psychic defences as standard. I imagine a race as well travelled as the Eyeless know all about the Time Lords.'

'No. They haven't heard of you,' Alsa told him.

That burst the Doctor's balloon. 'Oh... really?'

'They just asked something stupid. They – all right, all right, I'll ask – Doctor, they want to know if your TARDIS is a time machine.'

The Doctor felt his grin twitching. 'Er... no. Ridiculous idea.'

'The Eyeless would very much like a time machine,' Alsa said.

'I bet they would,' the Doctor murmured through gritted teeth.

'And you say you're a Time Lord and told Dela that TARDIS stood for Time And—'

'Oh. Right. Yes, I see why there's all this confusion. Simple mistake. It's "Thyme", with an H-Y. The herb. I'm a Thyme Lord. In the Middle Ages, you'd put some thyme under your pillow to ward off nightmares. Not that I've been to the Middle Ages, of course. Heaven forfend. You'd need a time machine for that. As a, er, Thyme Lord, I know that it's good with roast chicken. And in biscuits. You wouldn't think so, but try it. Couple of tablespoons. I could go on for ages about Thyme.'

'Please don't.' The Doctor wasn't sure if that was Alsa, or the Eyeless speaking through her. Either way, he sighed with relief. 'The Eyeless fail to understand why this means your brain needs such an elaborate firewall.'

'Isn't it obvious?' the Doctor said, then hesitated for a long while, before adding, 'It's because we don't want anyone stealing our recipes.'

He smiled, a little uncertainly.

'They believe you,' Alsa said, not bothering to conceal her dissenting opinion. 'They want your recipes. They don't just take stuff. They take experiences. Thoughts and emotions and fantasies. That's what the things suspended in their bodies are for – souvenirs. Badges.'

'Proof of individual achievement in a hivemind,' the Doctor muttered.

'The rules… they're dead complicated. If an Eyeless is the first one ever to feel or do something or go somewhere, it can wear a memento of it.'

The Doctor looked between the three aliens, tried to guess what each of the artefacts symbolised. Another Eyeless stepped out of the gloom, turned its head so it was facing the Doctor for the first time. The Doctor looked up at it. He took a deep breath.

'You're like me,' Alsa said, this time to the Eyeless, proudly pointing to a ribbon on her jacket. 'I earned that when I beat Hlann in a fight. Broke his nose. It's still wonky. You get what you want. That's like me, too.'

'This particular Eyeless does have eyes,' the Doctor told her.

Alsa had kept her distance, but now she was straining to see.

'Don't,' the Doctor warned softly. Then, twirling around to look back at that Eyeless, taking another step over, he said, 'Mr Eyeless… those ships of yours are very advanced. I mean, just one glance at them and it's obvious they have galactic range and they're powered by an artificial sun. Very few civilisations get so advanced. The people of Arcopolis are children by comparison. Well, Alsa is only 13, I suppose, so she's got an excuse.'

'Hey!' Alsa snarled, instinctively moving closer to the nearest Eyeless.

'You seem very pally with them, Alsa.'

'I can hear their thoughts. They can hear mine.'

'And you're birds of a feather?'

'I've no idea what that means.' Strange colourful, flappy thoughts appeared in Alsa's mind, placed there by the Eyeless. She ignored them.

'This one killed Jall. Did you realise that, Alsa?'

'Sure. He's wearing her eyes.'

He'd assumed she hadn't seen. 'Doesn't that bother you?'

Alsa shrugged. 'I understand why he did it. Can't put it into words... they're not like us. And I never really knew Jall that well. They operate on a bigger scale.'

The Doctor looked puzzled. 'Did you think that, or did they think that for you?'

Alsa frowned. 'I thought that,' she insisted.

'Of course you did.'

'Of course I did. Look, back at the Council, you were the one going on about the bigger picture. It's a shame Jall died, but rather her than me.'

'What makes you think that's the choice?' the Doctor asked.

'I don't come from a planet with choices.'

'We'll see about that.' He turned to the Eyeless with Jall's eyes. 'Those ships are very pretty.'

The Eyeless stayed where it was, let the Doctor come level with it.

The Doctor waved a hand above his head in the vague direction of the ceiling, took another step, turned to back into the wall. 'But this Fortress is very ugly. It's horrible. Offensive. At the moment, it's... well, it's asleep. Do nothing to wake it. Please, please do nothing to wake it.'

His other hand found the door frame.

'He's trying to get away!' Alsa shouted.

She really was very smart.

The Eyeless raised its right hand, held it straight out, pointing at the Doctor, palm flat. There was a gold disc embedded there. It flashed with the light of the sun.

The Doctor shrugged when nothing happened. He tapped his lip with the sonic screwdriver, which he'd just taken from his coat pocket. 'A weapon which literally burns out the neurons. Smoke pours out of the nose and mouth. Doesn't work on me, just like your telepathy doesn't work on me. Now... you killed Jall and I made a promise about Jall, and I will honour it.'

He took a step back.

'Last chance, Alsa. Pick which side you're on.'

'You make it sound like we're playing a game.'

The Doctor looked her right in the eyes, saw nothing but contempt there. So be it.

'Alsa?'

'Yes, Doctor?' she said, sneering.

'Playtime's over.'

NINE

Before anyone could stop him, the Doctor took the last step back through the doorway. As he passed through, in one movement and without looking back, he turned, brought the sonic screwdriver up level with the nearest control panel, operated it, and made the heavy black metal door slam down.

The Doctor didn't stick around to see what happened next.

The Eyeless who'd been closest to him managed to lurch forward and catch the underside of the door, quickly twisted to hold it about halfway open. The door was inching down, and the Eyeless wasn't going to be able to hold it for long.

'Go!' Alsa was shouting to the others.

The Doctor was already a hundred paces away. He could hear Alsa swearing and yelling, but it was already getting faint and after a moment the sound cut off completely. It felt wrong to abandon her, somehow. That said, there was no indication the Eyeless would harm her – rather the opposite – and she was far safer stuck back there than in the depths of this place.

Alsa's comm was in the Doctor's hand, set to display all the internal defences of the Fortress. Within fifteen seconds it had saved his life by spotting a row of nozzles in the floor. They were designed to blast up jets of poison gas, and he'd have completely missed them. The simple motion sensor that would have triggered the trap was easily tricked by the Doctor using a sweet wrapper he found in his pocket.

There were dull clangs of solid glass against metal floor. Footfalls behind him. One Eyeless had got through, but only the one. The Doctor had to slow down a little to neutralise every trap. Unless there was another door he could close behind himself soon – and he couldn't see anything obvious on the plan – it would catch up with him.

The corridor curved down. There were a number of locked doors to either side, but he couldn't slow down, so didn't try them.

He avoided a trap designed to fire plastic straps to snare his chest like a boa constrictor. He left it live, and hurried away. Ten seconds later, the Doctor was gratified to hear it triggered, but also alarmed the Eyeless had been that close behind him. The glass man didn't breathe, so the trap wouldn't suffocate it, and it'd be free soon enough.

The Eyeless fascinated him. Did they know specifically about the weapon at the heart of this Fortress, or had they simply marked out Arcopolis as a potential source of advanced technology?

He scolded himself. They must know. It was a long way to come on a whim.

He had to get to the weapon before the Eyeless did. No: faster than that. He needed to get to the weapon before they even tried, because when they tried… well, that would set the Fortress going and make his life difficult.

The Doctor picked up his pace.

If the Eyeless knew about the weapon, he wondered, did that mean they knew all his secrets?

Whatever the Doctor had done to the door, the Eyeless couldn't undo. There had been no way to brace it open, so there was only time for one Eyeless to get through. This frustrated Alsa, who kicked and punched at the metal, but all it did was clang and hurt her fists and feet.

That only made Alsa more angry.

The two Eyeless left behind stood there, unmoving, impassive.

'Don't you ever get upset?' she asked them.

'No. All our decisions and actions are rational.'

Alsa barged into the door, shoulder first. 'Damn it!'

'You will not open the door using that method.'

'You don't get it, do you?'

'No. I would like to.'

It was just the one with the eyes talking to her now, she could tell that somehow. It was almost like it was whispering to her. The other one was keeping its distance.

'I thought you could read my mind.'

'That does not mean I can feel what you feel. I would like to.'

And now Alsa was looking at herself standing over by the door. She felt confused, but didn't look it. She looked gleeful. That girl wasn't her. It looked like her, but... she was inside the Eyeless. She was tall, strong. She wasn't hungry or cold, wasn't even breathing. She could see right through her six-fingered hand. There was a gold disc in there. It was weird. She wasn't looking out through little holes in her skull, like she usually did; she had a total awareness of her surroundings.

'We've swapped bodies?' Alsa asked.

'That is the simplest way of describing it, yes,' the girl opposite her said, mumbling and slurring a little, as if she wasn't used to having a tongue. 'We call it psychografting.'

It was like she was driving its body. The Eyeless was clearly driving hers, flexing the fingers, running them up and down her arm. It revelled in the sensation, wide-eyed.

'How bizarre ... arms ... fingers ... hair!'

'Watch where you're putting those hands,' Alsa warned.

The other Eyeless shifted its feet, fascinated.

For the first time in her life, Alsa felt calm.

'You've never been angry before?'

'Not like this. Not the actual emotion, just a copy.' The Eyeless in her body was breathing hard, swaying. 'Such rage,' it said.

'I told you I was angry.'

'It is exhilarating. All sorts of hormonal surges and physical responses. I see something, I want to hurt it.'

'But that's what I see. All the time.'

In response, the Eyeless punched the wall, then grabbed at that hand with the other, crying out in pain. Alsa would have smiled, but the face she wore was featureless, immobile, so she couldn't. She looked down at her own arm… her new one. Alsa couldn't see herself inside the glass. A thought crossed her mind: where *was* she?

Never mind that: she really wanted to see how much she could wind up the Eyeless.

'The Doctor lied,' she said. 'All that stuff about herbs was rubbish. He let me down and he lied to you.'

'How can you be certain?'

'Normal people have intuition. Feel it in our stomach. Try it.'

The Eyeless growled, a noise that made Alsa start, even in her new, impassive body. She had never made that sound herself.

'The Doctor tricked me!' it snarled.

'Yes. He tricked us both.'

'I will kill him!'

The Eyeless slammed into the door then tried clawing at the metal. Its comrade watched this, impassively.

If it carried on like this, it would hurt itself. No, not itself: that was her body it was wearing, and Alsa wanted it back in one piece.

'You need to calm down a bit. Focus. You want to hurt him, not yourself. Close your eyes,' Alsa suggested.

She figured that closing eyes was something the Eyeless could never have done before, and she quickly felt the alien's mind grow almost giddy at the darkness.

'That is… so strange.'

'It's just normal.'

'No ... strange.' It was opening and closing its eyes, now. Grinning like an idiot.

After another minute of that, the Eyeless announced it would restore control of her body and Alsa was back where she belonged, feeling dizzy and her hand was throbbing. Alsa felt upset again, but it was dying down, becoming dulled. She wore the grin the Eyeless had made.

'We cannot allow the Doctor to escape,' the Eyeless said. Now it seemed to be both of them speaking again.

'We've got to be careful,' Alsa reminded them. 'The Doctor said that the Fortress was asleep, and we shouldn't wake it.'

'He said it was on standby,' the Eyeless concurred. 'We should also take into account that, while the Fortress demonstrates great potential, and warrants full investigation, we have what we originally came to this planet for.'

'You do?'

'We have the hypercube.'

The information poured into Alsa's mind, like she was remembering it. A hypercube was an object where the interior measurements were larger than the exterior ones. Like going into a small tent and finding that inside it was a huge hall.

Alsa got a mental picture of a big, blue, wooden box, with windows and a light on top.

'I don't recognise that at all,' she said, annoyed that they expected her to know about it.

'It is not Arcopolis technology.'

'Then… ?' she asked, impatient.

'We were passing through this space sector when we detected the hypercube in flight. We were able to calculate its trajectory to this planet and arrive here two days before it. It landed on a beach around ten miles from here and our landing party took possession of it shortly afterwards. Despite our efforts, we are currently unable to unlock the door. It remains on the beach where we found it.'

'Whose is it, then?'

'Ours,' the Eyeless said, confused by the question.

'Whose was it before? Where did it come from?'

'We think it belonged to the Doctor. We think it is the TARDIS he spoke to Dela about. While he did not describe its physical properties to her, he explained that the noun was an acronym for Thyme… Time And Relative Dimension In Space. Hypercubes possess the property of relative dimensionality.'

What flowed into Alsa's head next made no sense to her. It was a string of numbers and other symbols that might have been numbers, but none that Jeffip had ever taught her. The word 'equations' swam through her mind.

'I'll take your word for it.'

'We will learn all the secrets of the TARDIS.'

'What does the Doctor use it for?'

'Apparently it is a vehicle and a home and a museum and a laboratory and a library.'

Alsa was trying to get everything straight. So, the Eyeless had come to this planet looking for that big blue crate, the TARDIS. They weren't here for the weapon at all. They might not even know about the weapon.

'Weapon?' For the first time when it was in its own body, Alsa felt the Eyeless radiate an emotion: fear. Then another: fascination.

The Fortress strategy computer was assessing the pieces of data it had collected.

There were two alien creatures and a native humanoid in one of the outer chambers. They hadn't moved for a few minutes. The aliens communicated via simple telepathic broadcasts, which operated at 93.7 megamyers. The computer listened in, rather than jamming the signal. There were four more aliens outside, by the breach, and six native humanoids. An alien and a non-native humanoid were through the outer defences, heading to the central vault. There were three spacecraft immediately outside.

The computer sifted this information. There were two points of immediate concern.

The three spacecraft were potentially a threat. The strategy computer was watching them carefully. It toyed with the idea of a first strike, but rejected it. It was programmed to use proportionate force.

The non-native humanoid, the one with two hearts, concerned it more, because he had managed to get further than the strategy computer had originally projected. He was the one who had opened the outer hatches, using a sonic resonator. His avoidance of the various traps and snares indicated high levels of intelligence and initiative.

It checked its files, and discovered whole dedicated sections and subroutines about this individual, the Doctor. It brought them online, studied them.

The Doctor was aware of the weapon. He was making his way towards it. The computer selected the best strategy to stop him and implemented it.

This whole planet was quiet in the first place and the thick walls of the Fortress acted to provide soundproofing against even the silence. On the other hand, because it was constructed almost entirely of metal, every noise the Doctor made as he hurried through the latest corridor rang out and echoed. It was dark, with just the emergency lighting. The various traps that had dogged him at first were becoming increasingly thin on the ground and this worried him.

The Eyeless must have got out of the snare by now, although the Doctor hadn't heard it behind him.

He'd been moving for half an hour. There was still some way to the central vaults, according to the comm. The narrow corridors were a maze, like a nervous system or an animal warren – lots of tunnels branching off and leading to chambers and alcoves. The whole place was empty. There were racks and hooks and sockets everywhere, but no equipment or other material.

The immense strength of the weapon, even when it was inactive, was as tangible to him as the weather was when he was outside. He could feel its weight, oppressive.

The corridor opened up in front of him. It was now twice as wide, although this didn't serve an obvious purpose. For no reason he could have explained, the Doctor glanced down at the comm.

HELP

He looked back up. A beautiful face was looking right into his eyes. A ghost, standing in front of him, its cold, crisp glow radiating like nothing else in the perpetual gloom. It wore the same flowing white robes as the other ghosts he'd seen, and it looked just as scared, trapped. The ghost moved its hand, and the Doctor was going to take it, but then remembered what had happened to Frad.

It's not trapped, it's the trap. Don't forget that, Doctor.

'And I was just thinking how thin on the ground the automatic defences had become,' he said out loud. He glanced behind him, double-checking the Eyeless wasn't there.

The ghost looked bewildered.

The Doctor raised an eyebrow and tried the comm's keypad.

TIOUCH ME I DIEE

The Doctor was all thumbs, but the ghost got the message and took a step back. This was odd. If it really wanted to destroy him, it could have made a good stab at it. Why wasn't it trying? What reason could it have to delay? For that matter, why wait until the corridor was as wide as this and it would be easier to duck past? The Doctor peered at the ceiling to see if there was some sort of emitter or lens projecting the image. The ghost itself was gesturing around impotently. Its fingers brushed the comm.

IM LOOKING 4 SOME1

The Doctor was unused to this form of communication, so it took a moment for him to translate. This was an illusion, just a phantom generated by the Fortress. A defence system. A hologram – or something very like it –

with just enough artificial intelligence to work out where the chinks in his armour were. A lure. A trick.

What if he was wrong, though? It was an odd trick. He typed, fumbling a little.

I CAN HLP U

He thought for a moment, then added:

IAM DR? BTW

?????

It asked.

'I wish I knew,' the Doctor said, typing, ALIEN 4TRESS. IT ATTACKED ARCPLIS. He frowned, adding, U TRAPPED HERE?

The ghost nodded, frantic.

HELP FIND HER

The Doctor was about to ask 'who?' but the ghost anticipated this and added: DELA

'You know Dela?'

The ghost nodded, eager.

'I know Dela,' he said. The ghost understood the meaning without the Doctor having to type it out, and its face flickered with hope, for the very first time.

'What's your name?' the Doctor asked.

He read the answer.

'No. No, no, no.' The Doctor stepped back. 'This is a trap. This is still a trap. A very weird, extremely indirect… non-trappy… trap.'

There was a single word on the screen.

GYLL

'You're Gyll?'

Y

Dela's lover, the one she'd been so reluctant to talk about, killed on the day the Fortress appeared along with 200 million other people in Arcopolis.

U V BEEN HERE 15 YRS?

The ghost frowned, looked around.

15 MINS MAX

BUT 15 YRS SINCE ATTACK

N

Y

N

YYY WKO

?

WITH KNOBS ON, the Doctor clarified.

Gyll looked very lonely. Sad, more than panicked, like the universe had slipped through those ghostly fingers.

This is a trap, the Doctor reminded himself. A simple trick designed to feed back and magnify his fears and insecurities. Giving him someone to save, allowing him to picture the satisfaction he'd feel when he looked Dela in the eye and said he was sorry Jall died, but he had brought someone else back. The sort of small, human moment he lived for.

It might not be a trap. This might be Gyll, somehow not dead.

He could hear footsteps behind him – the Eyeless was close by. Impossible to tell how close.

The Doctor pulled himself together. The ghost was a distraction. Whether this was a trap or not, whether it was Gyll or not, it was still a distraction. The Doctor knew his priority had to be the weapon, not this.

The weapon could perhaps be altered so that it—

The Doctor didn't even allow himself to finish his thought. No.

I WILL COME BACK 4 U, the Doctor typed quickly, aware as he did so that he'd made a similar promise to Dela. He added a little more, until it read, I WILL COME BACK 4 U + DELA.

Then the Doctor swept past, careful to avoid even the slightest physical contact with the ghost. He didn't look back as he hurried away, so didn't see that Gyll was watching him go, tearful.

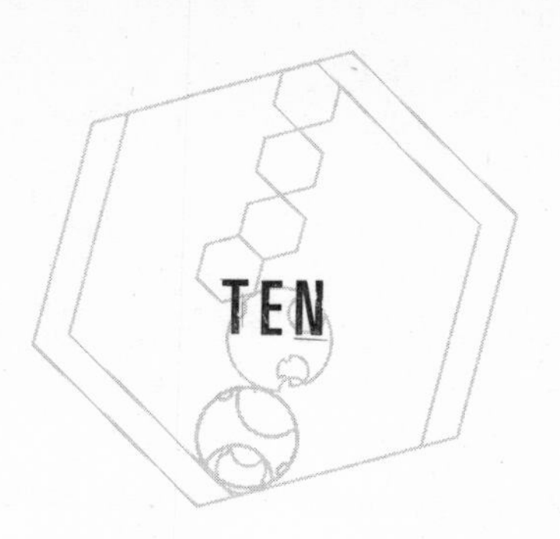

TEN

Alsa was working with the Eyeless with green eyes, trying to remember everything the Doctor had said about the weapon.

It told her that Dela had fought the telepathic process, found it unpleasant and intrusive. Alsa liked the feeling of having the Eyeless in her mind. Despite that, Alsa wasn't used to giving. She was used to cooperating, ganging together and divvying up the spoils. Kids did that when they had to. There was plenty for everyone, usually. But you always got something in return for helping someone. It was only fair.

The Eyeless said it understood, and now, suddenly, Alsa remembered running across a dusty, airless landscape, weighing almost nothing, leaping forwards a hundred metres at a time, kicking up bronze dust and being flooded with such an amazing elated feeling. Thirty Eyeless were around her, all sharing that feeling, amplifying it by endlessly feeding it back, running for running's sake.

'You actually did that?'

'Yes.'

'It's brilliant.'

'There was a danger we would be dashed against the rocks.'

'That was what made it brilliant. You could have died.'

'An unlikely outcome,' it told her before conceding, 'although a possible one.'

Reluctant to be dragged away from those memories, keen for more like it, Alsa remembered what the Eyeless wanted her to do. Alsa remembered the Council meeting, knowing exactly what Jennver was going to say because it was what she always said, letting the smelly old woman walk into it.

The Eyeless seemed more interested in that than in her memories of the Doctor.

'You were angry.'

Alsa snickered. When wasn't she?

The Eyeless were better than people. They could do so much that people couldn't. Jennver and the other parents wanted everyone to sit around eating weeds, plopping out babies. Alsa had thought the Doctor would change things, but he wasn't going to help her. But she wanted more than memories – if the Eyeless took the weapon, she couldn't use it to power the city—

'In return for your help, we will give you an engine that will do that,' the Eyeless promised.

'Will I be able to operate it?'

'Yes. We will give you that knowledge, too.'

'Only me?'

'That is your desire, so yes.'

'Give me another memory,' she said.

Jall screaming, terrified and alone as the Eyeless killed her, drank her thoughts so that it was both the murderer and the victim, the emotion feeding back, just like the sense of elation had a moment before.

Alsa's chest heaved like her heart was going to burst out of it. She felt terrified, but still not quite fully back in her own body. She was now acutely aware of the weight of her feet, the sweat in her armpits, the dryness in her mouth. Her breathing. She was breathing too fast. She had to stop breathing. Her tongue almost choked her.

'Why did you show me that?' Alsa gasped.

Jall's dead eyes peered down at her.

It was only a sensation, like the others.

Was that her own thought or had the Eyeless put it there? It wasn't anything like what she wanted to think.

'Not a nice sensation.'

'No. Neither good nor bad, merely true.' It hesitated. 'You want power over others, but why? Do you think you will be a good leader?'

Alsa shrugged. 'Don't you want to have power among the Eyeless?'

'No.' But the only Eyeless with eyes had paused, just for a moment.

'I suppose,' she conceded. 'Jennver got out of having babies. She's too old now, but she wasn't fifteen years ago. I want that choice.'

'Jennver holds the power in the village because she is the only obstetrician. You need someone to deliver the babies.

She has not shared her knowledge because that knowledge is her power.'

That simple truth had never once occurred to Alsa, but there was no disputing it. Jennver had been as manipulative as anyone. She almost felt admiration.

Alsa's mind now flooded with a whole new vocabulary: words like gravidity, macrosomia, haematocrit, folate, even somatomammotropin. More years' experience than she'd lived.

'You are now an obstetrician,' the Eyeless announced.

'What would you like in return?'

'Your anger.'

The thick steel door slammed down in front of the Doctor like a guillotine blade, almost taking his toes off.

Symbols set in the door explained it would stay deadbolt sealed for precisely one minute. Sensors dotted around the room whirred and bleeped. The Fortress was performing a full bioscan on him. This didn't worry him; it meant he must be getting closer to the weapon chamber.

The Doctor kept aiming glances over his shoulder, wondering how far behind him the Eyeless was. He'd not seen or heard it for a while. It might have been caught in another trap. Perhaps it had met the ghost.

The encounter with Gyll had rattled the Doctor. It didn't make sense that the ghost had been one of the automatic defences. Or, rather, it didn't make sense to him. If it was one of the defences, by definition there was a mechanical, perfect logic involved.

The Doctor wasn't sure what worried him the most:

that it was all part of a game the Fortress was playing with him and he didn't understand the rules... or that he'd really met the ghost of Gyll.

He'd met ghosts before. That didn't bother him. They were usually trouble, but plenty of the people and things and people-things the Doctor met on his travels were trouble.

No.

The thing was... the weapon, the ultimate weapon at the heart of the Fortress, utterly annihilated its target. The whole point of it was that it left no trace. If that was a real ghost, it was most certainly a trace. Not just something it had missed, something it had affected.

The Doctor didn't want to think too hard about the weapon; he wanted to get to it, destroy it and leave. Keep it simple.

The Doctor glanced down at Alsa's comm, but the screen was dead. He rattled the device and the plan of the Fortress reappeared, but as it did so, the floor shook.

That was puzzling. Had he really – ? He rattled the comm again.

The floor shook again.

'Am I doing that?' the Doctor asked out loud, wondering how he possibly could be.

Then he looked more closely at the display. It wasn't him – the Eyeless ships had begun their attack.

This wasn't good.

The minute was up, there was a click, the deadbolt slid back, and the door in front of him started to roll open, very slowly.

There was still no sign of the Eyeless. The Doctor glanced back — and something the size of a man, coiled and glinting, barely visible, was springing at him.

A poised landing and two sharp strides and the Eyeless was at him, swinging its arm precisely, efficiently. The Doctor's reflexive, panicky dodge worked, though, and the glass hand grasped at air.

The Doctor lurched for the door, but it wasn't far enough open, and he merely clanged into it.

'Get them to call off the attack!' the Doctor shouted at the Eyeless, ducking clear of another swipe.

It wasn't listening. It was hunched down, like a prize fighter, and had managed to get him to take two paces away from the door, which was now almost fully open.

The Doctor had to get out of here.

His opponent was used to reading minds, but couldn't do that now. So the Doctor simply feinted, moving to step right, then darting left, past it and through the doorway. The door slammed down between them.

Timelocked, deadbolt sealed. One minute.

The Doctor took a deep breath and hurried on.

Jeffip watched the four Eyeless who'd stayed out of the Fortress.

Fladon, Dela and the boys were at the big window, looking out at the spacecraft. Jeffip could hardly blame them for that. He, though, was far more interested in the ships' builders.

Telepaths. They'd taken memories from Dela, as easily as if they'd overheard her talking.

What sort of society would a race of mindreaders have? Jeffip thought of all the things they couldn't do: lie, cheat, boast, patronise, deceive, conceal, exaggerate, bluff. Those all seemed like negative things, and usually they were, but even the white lies, even being polite, would be impossible.

Jeffip didn't like the idea of living in a place where every passing thought was transmitted to everyone else. He had lived with the same three dozen adults for fifteen years, in a situation that forced them together, sharing so much. Even now, though, he didn't know absolutely everything about any of them. They all had secrets. He often thought things he didn't really mean, or had opinions he didn't want other people to know, or ideas he wasn't ready to share.

Jeffip was at a huge disadvantage. The Eyeless knew what he was thinking, but he didn't have a clue about them. He couldn't even work out *where* they thought. They didn't have brains, at least not like human beings did, or built-in computers or… well, anything he could imagine which was capable of thinking.

The Eyeless were wandering around and looked aimless, but Jeffip thought there must be some alien purpose to it. They could be pacing out the room, or performing some other type of survey.

One of the Eyeless was walking up to him, now.

'What are you looking at?' it demanded.

This startled Jeffip. Up until now, their voices had been perfectly calm.

'I meant no offence,' Jeffip insisted, looking down at his own feet.

'You like looking at people?' it asked.

Dela was near to them, and she walked over, puzzled.

'Why's it doing that?' she asked.

Jeffip shrugged.

'It's like it's drunk,' Dela pointed out.

It was a good description. The body language was different – more of a swagger.

'We need to get out of here,' Jeffip said.

'It's too risky to stay,' Dela agreed.

Something had changed, and Jeffip tried to think of the most diplomatic way of asking. Then he realised that the Eyeless had read his mind.

'We consulted our colleague,' it answered. 'The presence of a weapon of such power changes the equations. We have decided on a strategy of violent conflict resolution. Do not attempt to leave this area, as we will have further need of your knowledge.'

The calm way that was announced infuriated Dela, who just turned to Jeffip and looked like she was going to take it out on him. Jeffip was equally frustrated. He pushed his way in front of the Eyeless nearest to him.

'Careful,' Dela warned.

'The Doctor warned us,' Jeffip said curtly. 'You know that already.'

The Eyeless didn't respond.

'You would attack the Fortress?'

'The assault will begin shortly. Please take cover.'

They'd all heard that. Fladon and the boys looked around and quickly concluded that the safest place would be behind the engine blocks.

Dela joined Jeffip. He wanted to slap her, even though he knew she agreed with him that attacking the Fortress was insanity. What was the matter with him?

'I can't allow it,' Jeffip said, venting his anger on the Eyeless. 'I will do everything I can to stop this.'

The Eyeless raised its right hand.

Jeffip frowned. There was a gold disc embedded in the glass palm. Everyone noticed it at the same time. The ground had started to shake beneath their feet.

'I don't understand,' Jeffip said, irritated. 'What do want me to—?'

The gold disc flashed as bright as the sun for a fraction of a second. Jeffip staggered one step back, then stumbled over. Smoke was pouring from his mouth and nostrils. He tried to pull himself up, tried to cough, but instead all he did was die.

The Doctor wasn't worried too much about the Eyeless ships. He was extremely worried about how the Fortress would respond to them. He could see from the comm display that the Fortress strategy computer was running detectors over the spacecraft, as they moved into attack position. There was only one reason a strategy computer collected data.

He had to get to the weapon, and he had to do it right now, while the Fortress was still inactive, because things were about to get a lot more dangerous. The route was laid out for him, right there on the comm screen.

The Doctor began running.

***

Dela's eyes were screwed shut.

She was huddled with the others, behind the stack of engine blocks. They shouldn't have come here. It was so stupid of them. They told the children over and over not to come to the City at all, but especially not to go near the Fortress. Here they were, ten metres away from it. If they'd stayed in the village, what would have happened? They'd have just lost a few of the boys and Alsa, the biggest problem case amongst the girls. Jeffip would still be alive. The Doctor and the Eyeless would have settled their dispute without them – it wasn't as though any of the survivors could have changed anything.

'What's happening?' Morren said, so softly she hardly heard him, even though her son was curled up, pressing into her. Even with her eyes closed, Dela's world filled with light.

And then came the sound.

It was so tempting to turn and look. To fight that, Dela imagined her feet had been nailed to the floor and her eyelids had been gummed up with glue. It was the first time in years she'd had her two sons with her like this. The boys were holding – squeezing – her hands. She hoped she could transmit strength to them. Dela hoped she had that strength within her to give.

There was terror, like a blanket, numbing her, isolating her from the outside world. She tried, and failed, to block out the whole universe.

The ground was vibrating. A sensation Dela remembered from *before*, so she concentrated on that, the past, when the machines and engines of Arcopolis thrummed all the time, never sleeping, never even pausing. Every day since, Dela had had moments when she'd pictured the faces of her parents, her friends, her lover. There weren't any tears now, not after so long. She had also pined for the comforts of the city, the auto-massaging-showers, the instant food, pills that made headaches go away, robots that unloaded the washer-dryer and ironed everything. The humming now was different; a far less specific memory, one of a sense of activity, the feel of technology. It made her nostalgic, even as she felt scared that the light and sound coming from the Eyeless ships would take her apart. She'd been safe, then.

Dela used to get her music player to record the birdsong from outside, pipe it through to her when she was awake. The dawn chorus. She'd not thought about birdsong for years.

Did that mean her life was flashing in front of her eyes?

No. She was squatting down, somehow both terrified and numb. Alive.

Dela remembered the tiny suns hanging below each ship, and imagined them blasting out solid beams of energy, all aimed at the same spot on the side of those thick black Fortress walls.

The light and sound snapped off. She opened her eyes, discovered she was dazzled anyway, her eyes swimming with afterimages.

Fladon was saying something. Dela's ears were ringing so much she couldn't make out the words.

Cozzan was on his feet, looking back over at the Fortress. She tugged at his sleeve, but he was speaking.

'...ight. Stopped.'

Dela stood and looked. The attack had been so concentrated that none of the Factory's windows had broken. The air, though, felt like it was *hissing*. It must have been ionised or... Dela didn't have the vocabulary. She looked over at the body lying there on the factory floor. Jeffip would have known the words.

'We have to leave,' Fladon said.

'They said they would kill us.'

'They're too busy. We have to... to... take our chances.'

Three of the Eyeless were moving back over to the Fortress. Beyond them, through the window, high above, the alien ships were lined up. It might have been her imagination, but Dela thought the spheres beneath them looked dimmed, diminished. A quick look at the Fortress, and there was no obvious damage from this side, although there was a rusty, smoky smell.

The fourth Eyeless hadn't moved. Dela was level with it, could see the reflection of her face stretched and mapped onto it.

'Attack ineffective,' the Eyeless said. 'We anticipate a counterattack.'

The Doctor followed the directions the comm gave him: running a hundred metres, sharp right turn, first left. He'd just come to the end of the last corridor, taken his first step into the inner vault. It was almost pitch black, a great, cold, echoing place, bigger than a rocket silo or the biggest cathedral or even the hangar deck of a carrier ship. The Doctor – who was very good at seeing in the dark – had trouble making out much detail. He was about halfway up it, feet planted on a narrow metal walkway. He could just about make out that the huge space was crisscrossed with other walkways, as well as thick power lines. Below him were more gantries and power lines, and networks of metal pipes, discs and tubes. There were large shapes that were indistinct but loomed in the gloom.

The rumbling noise had stopped. The Fortress was no longer shaking. The Doctor checked the comm, but the map and directions had gone. In their place, the display flashed frantic warning icons over an image of a very small area of the Fortress wall, zoomed in for a second or two. There wasn't much damage and the image zoomed out again.

Klaxons and sirens started sounding. For three seconds or so, the Doctor assumed that he was the cause of the fuss, tensed and braced for an attack.

Then the Fortress changed.

Starting at the apex, taking about ten seconds, the interior of the Fortress lit up, one section at a time. This soft orange-white light marked out the vast space of the inner vault. A three-sided pyramid. Here were great galleries, staging platforms, empty hangar bays and docking cradles. They sat there in metallic layers, in rainbow steps and ledges of gold and silver and copper and iron and steel and bronze. They were connected by shafts and tunnels, but it was always possible to see at least one sloping black metal wall.

In the centre of the vault was a thick column, the core of the Fortress. It was a building within a building, and looking up and up and up at it, even the Doctor felt a vertiginous rush.

The column was battleship grey, about the same height as ten moon rockets on top of each other. It was thirty metres thick, so really quite slender, reaching from the ground right up to the top. With its hundreds of armoured branches, gantries and pipework, it looked a little like a great and ancient midwinter tree.

Right at the heart of it – and it seemed impossibly far away, now – was the chamber where the weapon was housed, waiting. The weapon chamber was a rough blip halfway down the central column, a pyramid pulled out of shape by the thick tangle of lines and cables. The Doctor could clearly make out a single long, straight walkway leading from the outer walls straight to the weapon chamber. That was about ten storeys above him, and the Doctor suspected it would be the most heavily defended route in the place. The comm was telling him there was a lift in the central column that would take him straight there.

The Doctor could hear sets of new traps snapping into place, all around, whole arsenals warming up.

The Fortress was awake.

There was a fresh hum very close by. A new system had come online. A quick check of the comm, and the Doctor could see that the Eyeless ships had the strategy computer's full attention. As yet, there was no sign that the internal defences were being ramped up. If elephants are stampeding towards you, it's not the time to worry about a little cold virus inside you.

'Bless you,' said the Doctor.

It was then that a glass arm whipped up and round his neck, so that a smooth elbow was level with the Doctor's Adam's apple, crushing the air from him.

ELEVEN

The Fortress made its move. The first blue energy bolt hit the middle Eyeless ship. Nothing happened. It fired a second, more powerful shot, which hit exactly the same spot. Nothing happened. The third energy bolt punched right through the hull of the ship.

Instantly, the Fortress brought half a dozen more turrets to bear, and they all fired, seven blue bolts hitting the breach in the hull, all from slightly different angles, at millisecond intervals. The bolts smashed seven different swathes through the interior structure of the ship, cracking open decks, igniting flammable items, rupturing power lines, causing chaos and explosions that quickly became chain reactions.

The Eyeless ship listed badly, but its crew was able to right it within moments. While they were doing that, the Fortress aimed all its detectors and peered through the holes it had made in the hull. It analysed the deck plans, weapons systems and engines. Within a second, the Fortress knew more about the Eyeless ship than its designers did.

Its attention turned to one of the other ships, the one on its right. This time, it only needed one shot, which hit at a seemingly random point on the underside. The glowing sphere hanging beneath the ship suddenly dropped like a stone, smashing down into the lake below, mere metres from the shore. It rolled a short distance, and the water beneath it instantly began boiling and steaming, and even caught fire.

The flames were smothered within seconds, as the rest of the Eyeless ship plummeted onto them. As the white hull touched the sphere, there was a flash of light and a huge explosion that blew a great crater into the soft earth. The shockwave toppled a couple of nearby skyscrapers. A mushroom cloud of pulverised mud, bits of Eyeless ship and steam slowly rose. A great wave in the lake sloshed and slurped against the walls of the Fortress. Tiny pieces of white hull material and what looked like small chunks of glass began showering down over a wide area.

The undamaged Eyeless ship fired seven small pulses of golden light from its sphere, each one hitting and ripping apart a gun turret.

The Fortress fell silent.

The damaged Eyeless ship drifted back a little. For the moment – as long as the surviving Eyeless ships kept where they were – they'd be safe, as the Fortress had no guns facing them.

This situation was unacceptable to the Fortress.

***

The Doctor had broken free of the Eyeless, but it still had a six-fingered handful of his coat and jacket lapel. The Doctor was close in, his arm under the Eyeless' so that he had it in what he rather hoped was a wrestling hold.

They were about halfway along a metal gantry made up of thin metal tubes. There was a doorway right at the end, leading into the central column. A little way from there was the lift that would lead straight up to the weapon chamber.

The Eyeless was making all the textbook moves, which made it easy for the Doctor to anticipate them. On the other hand, they were the textbook moves in the first place because they were effective. The net result was that the Doctor and the Eyeless were dragging each other along the gantry, almost waltzing, each trying to trip the other up without losing footing and tumbling off the gantry.

The glass man was clearly trying to calculate a countermove to break free from him. It had just occurred to the Doctor that, in theory, he should be able to communicate with the Eyeless using the psychic paper. The Doctor couldn't spare a hand to fish it out, and anyway the Eyeless would take its opportunity to attack him if he released his grip.

They got to the end of the gantry, into the lift and the door hissed shut behind them. The floor began to move.

It was a lift – that was all. It had been on the map, but from memory the Doctor had thought it had been a little further inside the central column, not right on its side. He'd be at the weapon when the lift stopped. Taking an Eyeless along for the ride hadn't been part of the Doctor's plan.

There were no nozzles or trap doors in the lift car, and it wasn't wired up to electrocute its passengers, but that didn't mean it was safe in here.

The glass man shoved the Doctor against the back wall. It wasn't any stronger than a human being, although that was strong enough to push the air out of his lungs. He recovered, twisted, managed to trip the Eyeless over. It was relatively light, and now he had it pinned, his knee in its back, although it was hard to keep hold.

The arm the Doctor had hold of was as clean and sharp as crystal, and had what looked like a little metal anchor embedded in it. Like a sailor's tattoo, the Doctor thought, unable to stop himself gasping out a laugh.

The Eyeless was trying to shake itself free. The Doctor gritted his teeth and kept holding it down. He wondered how brittle an Eyeless was.

There was a grinding sound beneath their feet.

They both looked down, puzzled.

Was the Fortress arming the –

The Doctor panicked. When two hearts start racing at once, it isn't a pleasant sensation. It sets the epinephrine flowing a bit too freely.

– weapon that killed Arcopolis?

'No,' he concluded out loud, calming himself down. 'No. This is something else.'

For a start, the weapon was above him, not below. So what was the noise? Even though he couldn't hear its thoughts, the Doctor could tell the Eyeless was asking itself the same question. It tugged, tried to stand. The Doctor didn't let go.

'If I knew,' the Doctor announced calmly, 'I would have been a bit more specific. Like I say, it's something else.'

The lights dimmed a little.

'They're diverting power to the... something else.'

The next creak and clatter was nearer still.

'Hang on...'

The Eyeless had loosened its grip a little.

'Let me use the comm,' the Doctor said. He used his free hand to retrieve it. 'The comm? See? Comm see, comme ça.'

The Doctor checked the screen as best he could without completely letting go of the Eyeless. To his relief, it clearly showed that the lift was heading up. It was just a few floors away from the weapon chamber, and...

Thing was, if the noises beneath them were getting nearer, that meant the lift was going down. Now the Doctor came to think about it, it did feel like the lift was falling.

'Oh,' he said, realising. 'The comm's been lying to me.'

He let that sink in for both of them.

'Well... to us, really,' he added. 'The Fortress hacked into the comm, fed me what I wanted to see, gave me a route that only said it was to the weapon chamber. All the time it was leading me here.'

The comm went dead.

Another grinding, puttering sound, which echoed like a cackle, inches beneath them, making the floor of the lift car thrum and vibrate.

'If we're going to survive, we need to cooperate,' the Doctor suggested. 'It's the rational thing to do.'

The Eyeless hesitated, then nodded. Slowly, the Doctor let go of it.

The Eyeless held out its hand, which the Doctor shook.

Then the door opened, the lift car tipped itself right over, and the Doctor and the Eyeless fell out.

They dropped, hands clasped, straight down through five metres of darkness, before crashing onto a metal surface. The Eyeless hit it chest first, with a sound like someone dropping a crate of beer bottles. The Doctor let go of its hand and it flipped over and slid away, lifeless, torso dashed to bits, down into the gloom.

The Doctor didn't shatter, but he did slide off, falling only a metre or so, but then going on to hit a ledge, rolling over that for a while, and then down another five metres, landing flat on his back on solid rock.

'Ow,' he noted.

There was a new sound. Metal against metal, a vast mechanism creaking into life. A great ratcheting noise, clanks and what sounded like bolts clacking back.

The Doctor had heard a sound like this before, and tried to place it. It rang a bell… and that phrase reminded him of the other day, the thing he'd been telling Gar and Alsa about. Being up in St Stephen's Tower, chasing the last of the Steggosians round the workings of Big Ben, dodging that spiky tail of his.

Concentrate. Concentrate on identifying the noise, the Doctor told himself.

And don't black out.

He'd heard this sound in London, but on a different occasion. Ages ago. Where and when?

'Tower Bridge!' he exclaimed, wincing at the effort. 'It sounds like Tower Bridge getting ready to open up.'

The Doctor, still flat on his back, soaked up the scene. He had an ideal vantage point. He was lying in a three-metre deep, ten-metre wide trench cut into what looked and felt like bedrock. The trench was very slightly curved. Above, all around, horizontal and vertical, was a great mesh of cogwheels, made of the same black metal as the walls, marked out with silver and grey rivets. There were drive shafts and pistons like redwood trees. There were flywheels the size of houses, drive belts you could have used as bus lanes.

Peering down past his feet, the Doctor could see an enormous drum, like the front of a steam roller. It was about a hundred metres away, so partially obscured by the curve of the trench. It was ten metres tall and just as wide, so rested perfectly snugly in the groove the Doctor was lying in. Above and to each side were vast numbers of cogwheels, belts and gears, all – eventually – connected up to the axle of the roller.

'Ah,' said the Doctor, who'd just worked out what it all did.

There was a creak, then a clank. A deep rumbling note, and the roller started edging forwards, towards him. It was moving at walking pace, so would reach him in about a minute.

All in all, this wasn't the best time to realise he couldn't quite get his legs to move. He'd just fallen about ten metres and landed spine-first on solid rock. The fact that he didn't feel any pain was not encouraging.

'This is a really inefficient and melodramatic way of killing one person,' the Doctor complained loudly. 'Even if that person is me.'

He looked back over at the roller, now fifty metres or so away from his feet. The grinding was deafening. The roller must have weighed hundreds of tons, easily.

'Although I have to hand it to you… it does look like it'll work.'

The Doctor could wiggle his toes. Using all his concentration and willpower, he knew he'd be able to move in another thirty seconds.

His main problem now was that the roller would reach him in twenty.

Hydraulics and great gears hissed and clanked around. Every cogwheel was turning. It sounded like the engine room of an ocean liner going full steam ahead. The heavy roller was a wall of metal, turning so very slowly, scraping and sparking against the bare rock, its rotation as unstoppable as a planet's. The Doctor had nothing but admiration for the engineers who'd designed and built such an incredible machine.

The edge of the roller brushed the tips of his trainers. The Doctor forced his feet to move, but they only twitched. He tried to throw them back over his head to flip himself upright. They only got halfway.

With a mighty hiss, the roller came to a dead stop.

The Doctor was bent into an L shape. His legs – had he noticed before quite how long and skinny they were? – pointed straight up in the air, the backs of them resting on the cold metal roller.

He was not only bent at a right angle, he was at exactly the right angle to see what had happened. By comparing the new position of all the mechanisms, he was able to work out what all that mechanical activity had been in aid of.

All this vast machinery at the base of the pyramid was dedicated to one purpose. It hadn't been to kill him. The Doctor now knew what the roller had been doing and why it had stopped.

'You're kidding,' the Doctor whispered.

The Eyeless ships had disabled the guns on the side of the Fortress facing them. The fighting was over, at least until the Eyeless attacked again. Barely controlled thoughts and concern about the many, many Eyeless casualties flitted between the four glass men out here.

Likewise, Dela and Fladon were over at Jeffip's body. There was a terrible truth about the future. Neither of them was ready to confront it so soon.

'What do we do with it?' Fladon asked, ever practical. They were a long way from the settlement. It would be hard enough just getting the body down to ground level to bury it out here.

Dela knew the sensible thing to do was to leave. There was nothing they could do here, on the front line of some interplanetary war. She'd stayed because she hadn't wanted the Eyeless to cut up Jeffip's body just so they could add a red eye and a blue eye to their collection.

Fladon took her hand, but she shook him away. Dela felt numb, detached from events.

An Eyeless swept past her, agitated. As she stepped out of its way, not wanting to antagonise it, a wave of anxiety passed over her. She had every reason to be worried, of course, but this didn't feel like it had come from within her. The emotions of the Eyeless were infectious. Was that why she had been feeling so angry before? She'd caught it from the Eyeless?

There was a crunch.

'What was that?' she asked.

The other humans were coming over, wary. The Eyeless closest to them was looking equally lost.

'It sounded like ice breaking,' Fladon said, aware it wasn't a helpful answer.

Another crunch.

'Where's it coming from?' Gar asked. They were all looking down at the floor.

'The attack must have weakened the Factory's foundations,' Fladon offered.

'Without even cracking the windows?' Gar sneered. The kids who came out into the city were all experts on the ways buildings collapsed.

Cozzan was looking around. 'That's weird,' he said.

'It's possible,' Fladon said, not hearing. 'When that ship hit the ground, it would have fractured the subterranean travel tunnels. The cracks could have spread.'

Morren was close, almost huddling. It was disconcerting for her son to treat her in this way, Dela realised, more than a little guiltily.

'Are we moving?' he asked.

'No...' Dela said quietly.

But they did seem to be turning, angling away from the solid mass of the Fortress. A memory. For the first time in fifteen years, Dela remembered what it was like to sit in a monorail carriage when it set off. It would look, for the first few seconds, like you were sitting still and the station was reversing away.

They all realised in the same moment it was the Fortress that was moving, not them.

The immense black wall was shifting. The whole Fortress was rotating on its central axis, as though it was mounted on gimbals. It was slow, about walking pace. It was unnerving, like watching a mountain turning to get a better look at something.

'The Factory is in its way,' Cozzan said.

Now the Fortress was twisting, grinding away the concrete and metal superstructure of the native building. It moved clockwise, exposing the side that had been buried in the Factory to the Eyeless ships.

The ceiling above them was creaking.

And now it was definitely time to get back to the village.

Dela, her children and Gar all ran, as the big window finally shattered and the floor beneath them began to ripple and moan. Sparks flew from the machines of the Factory production lines, giving up the final ergs of power they'd hoarded for fifteen years.

A minute later, with a triumphant, echoing slam, the Fortress stopped moving. Almost round the corner, now, Dela and her sons turned to see a black wall identical to the one that had been there before.

The Eyeless had stayed rooted to the same spot. They had been showered with debris from the shattered window and the wreckage that had fallen from the ceiling. Dela could see three of the four, and they didn't seem injured or damaged, or whatever the right word was, but the other was gone. Dead. Jeffip's body had been completely buried, possibly even crushed, and the other Eyeless must be under the rubble, too.

Fladon hadn't run, but had been thrown over as the Factory convulsed. Now he was getting up, coughing.

Stay still, Dela heard herself think. It was another warning from the Eyeless.

It came too late.

Fladon was blasted to pieces by a blue energy bolt.

The Doctor had buried the automatic gun, but on a wall that was now facing away from them. The new wall had a new turret.

Dela heard three Eyeless voices screaming warnings. Not to her, to their ships. She was already running, pulling all the children along with her.

The Fortress had turned itself 120 degrees and locked into place with a new side facing the Eyeless ships. The lake sloshed around its base, trying to settle down.

Fresh guns now faced the Eyeless. Ten of them fired, the energy bolts converging on the same spot on the sphere hanging below the undamaged ship. They punctured it, let it explode in mid-air.

The fireball enveloped the vessel above, burst it and then dispersed the remains on a shockwave that broke every window within a ten-mile radius but bounced harmlessly off the Fortress itself.

The last surviving Eyeless ship, the first to be hit, fired little golden pulses, intending each one to hit a turret on the Fortress. It had worked before, but now the Fortress was ready for the attack and it fired seven shots, each hitting an energy pulse, popping them. Then the guns fired a third time.

By now, the Eyeless ship had thrown up a force field, which absorbed most of the energy but couldn't stop the ship being flicked miles into the heart of the city, right into and among a cluster of skyscrapers.

The Fortress took no pleasure watching the Eyeless ship slamming into a tall tower, its masts toppling and the hull corkscrewing down to the ground. The ship flipped over as it fell, bounced off other structures, carved great gouges into the buildings, scooped out blocks of masonry. The Fortress was keeping a tally of alien life signs, and that fell to zero during this process, even before the bulk of the ship hit ground level.

The Fortress updated its records to register it had neutralised a threat.

As the ship's force field had failed, however, the ship's artificial sun had broken off – or been deliberately ejected – and was now hurtling towards the Fortress. The strategy computer detected this and had the automatic guns blast at it, but it had been caught off-guard, and wasn't able to get a good aim. It scored ten near misses. Ten energy bolts shot off in different directions, far into the morning sky. The ball of energy continued on its course.

The Fortress had no strategies to prevent the impact, and switched to damage limitation.

Alsa could read the mind of the two Eyeless, an ocean of resentment, rage and frustration.

'What's going on?' she asked.

'So many dead.'

'What? Who's dead?' Was it talking about Eyeless or real people?

'We are now in the line of fire,' it told her. 'The side facing the ----'

That last word hadn't come out at all. 'The what?'

The shockwave from the blast had already knocked them off their feet when the front wall shattered and hurled itself at them, so quickly Alsa didn't even have time to close her eyes. She saw the two Eyeless lifted off their feet and slammed into the back wall like dolls. Then all she could see was the slab of black metal that reared up off the floor and was about to hit her right in the face. A wave of heat washed over her, but everything was dark now.

The Doctor finally managed to summon the willpower to stand up. He hopped to his feet, trying not to cry out as he realised just how many bruises he had.

He knew there was no way he could scale the sheer side of the trench, and the metal of the roller was far too smooth to get a handhold.

He checked the comm. The three Eyeless ships had been destroyed. He could believe that, but he couldn't trust the comm with much else. So he tossed it up onto the ledge, stepped back, and used the sonic screwdriver to detonate its battery. That blew a metre-thick chunk of rock out, which fell into the trench, forming a rough set of steps. He clambered out, onto the floor at the base of the Fortress.

He pulled himself upright, twisting his aching shoulder round to see if that helped the pain. It didn't. He looked up. The weapon chamber appeared to be impossibly high above him. He was at ground level and virtually at the outer wall. He'd have to get across the whole of the floor to the central column, then climb up, somehow. The Fortress was awake now, all the defence systems online. The Doctor could feel it peering down at him, waiting for the moment to pounce. That little trick with the comm and the lift car demonstrated that the Fortress was far more than just a machine designed to kill an intruder, it was a machine designed to *enjoy* killing an intruder. Not because it liked being vicious, almost the opposite: it liked solving puzzles. Murdering him would satisfy the Fortress in the same way as it was satisfying to solve a crossword.

His foot scuffed against something solid. A glass head, with a great crack in it. The Doctor picked it up. It was light. Decapitated heads tended to be heavier than they looked, in his experience. This one was utterly inert, nothing to indicate it had ever been alive.

'One down,' the Doctor noted, carefully laying the head back on the rock floor.

He was trying to work out what to do next when a streak of golden light punched its way through the wall behind him, about a hundred storeys up. It looked like a small, squashed sun.

The Doctor made a run for it. This wasn't just to avoid the debris, which was already beginning to crash down around where he had been standing. It was also because the ball of energy was so bright, so powerful and such an immediate threat that it would both blind and occupy every sensor in here – for the next few precious seconds, at least.

Its light had seared an afterimage into the air itself, but almost all of its force had been spent getting through the walls. It managed to bore a hole in the tangle of walkways and cables, but all the sphere could do after that was splash feebly into the central column, like a blob of lava. It left a congealed splash of metal, like a sore, on the side of the column, and that was already cooling rapidly.

It posed no further danger to the Fortress. Which meant that the only remaining threat was the Doctor himself.

He gulped.

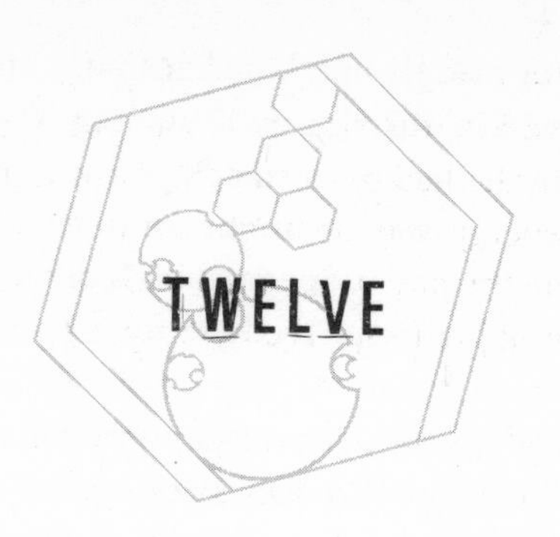

TWELVE

The winding corridor Alsa had come along with the Doctor to get this far into the Fortress was all gone, replaced by a sloping tunnel of jagged black metal. The explosion had burrowed hundreds of metres deep into the thick double walls. Sunlight streamed in through the gap, down past the stumps of sliced pipework and cables and through the five glass men standing there.

Alsa was already up. Her nose was a bloody mash, like someone had punched it. She was dabbing it with her sleeve. Apart from that, she was fine.

She felt the anger of the two Eyeless who'd been with her all this time, burning hotter than ever and hotter than her own. The three newcomers were offering to share their calm, simply paste over the negative emotions. The one with the green eyes was refusing, suggesting that they have his rage instead.

'Are you the only survivors?' Alsa asked.

There should be others – scouts and other patrols. None

of them were close enough for telepathic contact, though. They ought to be regrouping. It was known that many hundreds, all of the Eyeless on the ships and two down here, had died. There might only be these five.

Human beings had the expression 'their memory lived on', but it wasn't true, not really, it just meant that people remembered the dead. And it wasn't like the parents remembered everyone. The thirty-seven parents were just ordinary people. They had had friends and relatives – very small families back then from what they always said, ones with less than a handful of kids. Say they knew a thousand people, being really generous – this was a dizzying number of people for Alsa. Say, for sake of argument, they each 'knew' a different thousand people. They 'knew' a woman they passed in the street, or a neighbour they'd never talked to, or some shop assistant. That would mean that between all of them, they only remembered 37,000 people, out of all the people in Arcopolis.

The Eyeless did the maths: the parents only remembered around 1 person in 5,405. It was total oblivion for everyone else. Not even their names survived. They didn't even count as *strangers*.

It was different for the Eyeless. Their memories literally lived on, copied into the minds of the other Eyeless.

The Eyeless shared everything. There was no privacy, and Alsa didn't like that idea. She'd never liked people looking at her. She dressed in layers and layers of clothing, never went swimming when the others did, never told anyone else how she was feeling about stuff. That was for babies.

The Eyeless were better than people. Alsa had worked that out ages ago. They could do so much she couldn't. But it wasn't just that – they were so much more ambitious. All of the glass men here had done so many things. Wanting privacy felt silly. Childish. Still, a part of Alsa needed it. She felt a lot more comfortable thinking of their communication as a conversation, not a mingling of thoughts.

She wondered if they could still give her the engine they'd promised her. She hadn't said anything, but they knew she was thinking about that, and hadn't answered.

The Eyeless felt trapped now, alone, but they were practical, they were looking for a solution. Their telepathy only worked over a short distance. They couldn't call for a rescue ship with it. They needed a beacon.

Like the comm mast in the middle of the village, Alsa thought. She hadn't meant to volunteer that thought, but the Eyeless were already agreeing to commandeer it. As one, the five of them turned to go.

'Hang on! Don't you want this weapon?' she asked.

The Eyeless hesitated.

'Of course,' they said finally, in unison. 'It is also in our interest to ensure no one else has it.'

'The Doctor won't trade for it.'

'We cannot read his mind, so cannot say that for certain. You think we have to use force.' It wasn't a question, of course, as the Eyeless knew exactly what Alsa thought.

She pictured the scene: armies of Eyeless, surrounding the Doctor, arms raised, about to tear him to pieces. She asked them if the Eyeless would do that.

'Yes, if the stakes were high enough.'

'Well – are they?'

'If the Doctor is describing the weapon accurately, there is a dominating strategy: the weapon should be acquired at any cost up to, but not including, our total annihilation.'

Now the Eyeless were picturing the interior of the Fortress. Before the ships had been destroyed, they'd scanned the building. The five glass men and Alsa contemplated the results. Alsa could see where the weapon was – right at the heart of the pyramid – and she could see how to get to it. One walkway led straight there. Simple.

Except that she could also see the defences. Automatic guns and other systems that Alsa struggled to understand.

There was a flutter of excitement.

'What?' Alsa asked.

The impact of the miniature sun that had powered the last Eyeless ship had smashed a long, straight route through the interior of the Fortress. This had disrupted the defences. The Fortress had compensated – realigned various turrets and so on – but coverage wasn't perfect. There were a few blind spots.

It took Alsa a moment to interpret the images.

'There's a safe route through, now?'

No… but there was an area close to the weapon chamber with only one gun. It would be possible to follow a route along pipes and gantries, then drop down and run the last fifty metres.

'That's not so far,' Alsa thought. 'And that one gun?'

Could fire five times in that time, maintaining eighty per cent accuracy.

'If someone stepped onto that walkway, four times out of five they'd be killed?' Alsa asked, aghast.

No, they explained patiently. That would be true if it could only fire once. It could fire five times. If someone stepped onto the walkway, they'd be killed 3,124 times out of 3,125.

She didn't believe them, so they patiently talked her through the probabilities. They were right.

'That's the same as saying there's no way across!' she cried out.

There was always a solution, the Eyeless assured her. It was simply a matter of finding it. This was something to work with. Their best chance.

The Doctor and the Fortress were not locked in an epic struggle.

This would be over quickly. The Doctor would get to the weapon or the Fortress would kill him. This wouldn't be a game of chess; it would be more like a shoot-out. It felt to the Doctor like he was fighting a volcano… no, an ogre. A mechanical giant.

This thought heartened him a little, as he'd fought ogres and giant robots plenty of times in the past, and hadn't been beaten by one yet.

Then again, the bad guys only had to win once.

The Doctor had concluded that if he stuck close to the exposed mechanisms that had moved the Fortress around, it wouldn't be able to attack him with the really nasty stuff like high explosives or acids or even energy blasts. It meant he was running a very convoluted course to the central pillar, darting from one delicate piece of equipment to another, always careful to leave plenty of options for himself. He was still alive, obviously. So far, the defences had consisted of nothing but bursts of radiation that he could literally just shake off and little blasts of poison gas that were relatively slow and so easy to see coming.

A tiny dart nicked his hand as it whizzed past.

The Doctor didn't slow down, but had a quick look at the damage: a very light scratch that stung like a paper cut. He didn't like this. Not to say that he'd have preferred to have his hand sliced off, but… well, why just poke at him?

On instinct, he dived and rolled. A mini-missile shot straight over him. It was moving fast, but the Doctor could tell it was only about the size of a bottle of wine. It bobbed around making the distinctive buzzy, dopplered sound of an antigravity generator.

The Fortress fired a second mini-missile, which the Doctor leapt over like it was a hurdle. The weapon had anticipated the Doctor would duck, like he had the first time, so it had aimed low. Glancing back over his shoulder, the Doctor saw that both missiles were now arcing round to have another go.

He glanced down at his hand, with its tiny scratch.

The dart had taken his biodata sample.

The missiles were programmed with his genetic details, and wouldn't give up until they'd hit him.

Dela and the children were outside now and had finally stopped running. Dela's skin was tingling. It had only been when she saw Cozzan's red face that she realised they all had instant sunburn from the sphere that had broken off the Eyeless ship. Apart from that, she felt fine. The boys had no obvious injuries or distress. She was proud of how calm they'd been.

They had led her out of the Factory down to ground level and straight into an area thick with trees. The Fortress still overshadowed them, but they were shielded from the worst of the oppressive black shape by a canopy of fronds and ferns and flat leaves. Dela could barely see ten paces in front of her.

'It's the Urban Jungle,' Morren told her solemnly.

'A good place to get lost,' Gar said.

'Yes,' she said, looking back. She wondered if the Doctor was all right.

The ground was wet from the previous night's rain, and the air was saturated with the smells of loam and fruit and pollen and bark and so much else.

'What was it before?' she wondered aloud. They were east of the Factory, not all that far from where she'd lived. There had been nothing like this in the City back then.

The boys all approximated a shrug.

Dela tried to get her bearings. 'Close to the Aircar Factory, in the direction of the… it's the Botanical Gardens. No, too close, they were miles away… wait… the plants have spread out. Seeds and spores must have blown here.'

'There are domes and stuff in the heart of the Jungle, where the plants are thickest,' Gar confirmed, nodding his head in the right direction, keeping his hands in his pockets.

'Nothing's very colourful,' Dela said.

'What do you mean? It's all green.'

Dela laughed. 'I used to come here. Well, to the Gardens.'

'With, er, thingy?' Cozzan asked.

'Gyll, yes, and on school trips and with my parents before that. It was where rare plants were kept. There were flowers, then. Every size and shape and colour.'

The flowering plants would have survived the coming of the Fortress, but slowly died off without any insects to pollinate them. The vegetation no longer had to appeal to bees or ants.

'What are we going to do?' Cozzan asked.

Dela had been thinking. 'We go back to the settlement. Get out the way, let the Doctor and the aliens… the other aliens… settle their dispute.'

'I meant now Jeffip and Fladon are dead. They did so much.'

Dela hadn't thought her heart could sink any lower. She'd put that question to the back of her mind.

'They learned their skills. Boys like you will have to step up to take their place. We will all have to be braver.'

'You lived in the Jungle before?'

'No… it wasn't here, this was all just part of the city. I was a bank manager.'

'A what?'

She smiled. 'That would take a very long time to explain. Jeffip was a teacher. A primary school teacher. Fladon worked in the Car Factory. Very little of what we knew before was any use.'

'Mum!' Morren called out. He was a little way ahead,

and was now signalling them all to slow down.

The boys' feral instinct was to duck down. Dela craned her neck, hoping to get a better look at whatever it was. Gar grabbed at her.

Dela felt them in her mind before she saw them. Dozens of Eyeless, marching in single file, each of them negotiating the obstacles and hazards they encountered, ducking under branches, stepping over root bores and round fallen trees without breaking their stride or their perfect formation.

A burble of thoughts, imperatives and observations, flittered between the aliens. They were marching on the Fortress; were one of five groups heading there; wanted to get inside the building and acquire the weapon before the Doctor did.

If they saw the humans, or heard their thoughts, they didn't acknowledge it. The glass men were already hard to see, and within seconds of passing, the column had completely disappeared into the foliage.

'I have to warn the Doctor,' Dela said. No one was more surprised hearing the words than she was, but saying them had been a liberation. She knew it was the right thing to do. Then, she said to the boys: 'You can find your way back to the settlement? Do that. Warn Jennver and the others. Tell them what happened.'

She hugged them all, even Gar. That left them too embarrassed to object. Dela took her chance to escape them.

The two missiles were circling and had the Doctor pinned with his back to a large metal pillar.

They were in a circular vault, around seventy metres in diameter. The missiles were circling the perimeter of the room, sticking close together. There were ten exits, equally spaced, along the perimeter, but every time the Doctor made for one of the doorways, one of the two missiles started heading for it and they could travel four times faster than he could. The pillar he had his back to was a crankshaft in the middle of the room that the missiles didn't want to damage, so they were waiting for him to make his move. They didn't seem to want to come in any closer than the perimeter.

He had to get to one of the doors, but every time he started towards one, it became clear the missiles could get there first.

He was more than a little annoyed with himself, because there was clearly, mathematically, a way to get to a door. The Fortress was setting him a puzzle.

'Something to do with pi,' he told himself.

He waited until the missiles were directly behind him, then ran for it, straight towards one of the doors, but one of the mini missiles started powering round. He turned his head, and it was obvious that it would get to the door before he got anywhere near.

The Doctor ran back to the middle of the room, and the shelter of the mechanism there. The missile raced past the doorway before resuming its perimeter patrol.

'2 pi R,' the Doctor said, still trying to work out the solution. 'The radius of the circle is, um, call it a hundred feet... er, I mean thirty metres... and there's a value of... they're four times faster than me, so if I'm standing a quarter of the radius of the... I'm in the centre of the circle, so if I... but there are two missiles... so if I'm standing an eighth of the radius of... Oh, stuff this for a game of soldiers!'

In no mood to play along, he pulled out the sonic screwdriver and started running straight at the missiles. One of them pitched round and straight at him. There was no time to check, so the Doctor fired away and hoped he'd got it right.

A big glob of air shimmered in front him and the missile flew right into it. Instantaneously, every screw, weld, seal and rivet failed. The missile became a bucketful of missile components, not one of which was connected to another. The pieces also lost all their momentum, just drizzling down onto the ground.

For every action there was an equal and opposite reaction – in other words, the force of the sonic burst flicked the Doctor off his feet and sent him flying back. He landed on one foot, stumbled, fell and landed awkwardly. His body noted irritably that it was tired and bruised and scratched enough already, thanks.

Despite that, the Doctor felt like kissing the sonic screwdriver. There was a cloud to the silver lining: the Maximum Disassemble setting drained all its power. He could set the screwdriver to recharge itself, perhaps by absorbing ambient sound, but that would take a few minutes.

Which was a shame, as the second missile was coming straight for him right now.

It was moments away. Reflexively, the Doctor flinched

and raised his elbow so it was right between his head and the missile, peered at the weapon through the crook of his arm.

The air between them was blurring, growing opalescent.

The Doctor had just formed the thought that it might be a residual effect of the sonic burst when the shape resolved into a ghost – a middle-aged man in a toga, with a smooth head.

The ghost fixed a dark-eyed stare at the Doctor, surprised to see a man cowering quite so comprehensively from it.

The ghost didn't see the missile coming. The Doctor did, through its translucent, bald head. He wasn't sure what would happen, but couldn't do much to affect the outcome anyway. In the event, the missile hit the ghost square in the back of the head and the two were annihilated in a burst of light.

The Doctor blinked the flash out of his eyes.

'Oh, I am so sorry,' he murmured. It was pure luck that he hadn't been hit himself, but that didn't make him feel any better about it.

He scrambled around on the ground for something, found it and hurried off towards one of the doorways.

Before he got much further, his route was cut off by a shimmer in the air. Another ghost had appeared. Another one. Another. Within moments, there were too many ghosts to count – there was just a tornado cloud made from long limbs, flowing robes and hair, lit from within, engulfing him.

***

The Eyeless had been burbling away, crunching the numbers, drawing up their plan. Alsa stood between them all, but didn't feel involved. They were finally calming down. As was she, Alsa realised. Their emotions were catching.

The mental images of the inner vault held in the five Eyeless minds dripped details of the traps that lay in wait. The Eyeless had worked out that the Fortress would only ever hit back slightly harder than it had been hit. The Eyeless had confronted it with three ships. If they had brought thirty, it would have attacked them with ten times the ferocity.

'The Doctor was smart to show up here on his own, without any guns or other weapons,' Alsa said. 'He left his spaceship on the beach, so he's still got a spaceship.'

She was trying to rile them, but it wasn't working. The Eyeless understood she was impatient, so without waiting to be asked what her plan was, she told them they should let the Doctor do the hard work of getting the weapon, then ambush him. Simple.

'No,' the Eyeless said. It was like a chorus. 'It is not acceptable to allow anyone else even temporary control of the weapon. We have to acquire it first.'

'There's no way to do that,' Alsa complained.

'We have calculated an option that guarantees we can secure the weapon chamber before the Doctor arrives,' the Eyeless told her.

As one, they turned towards the corridor that led into the central vault.

'Are you going to tell me what it is?' Alsa demanded.

The corridor was uneven and blasted, making it tricky to follow them.

She saw their plan.

'That's it? Charge at the guns? It's suicide!'

'Not for all of us. The benefit justifies the cost.'

'You don't want to die, surely?'

'It is not our preference. Humans have adopted such strategies. Your current culture is based around short-term sacrifice to ensure the survival of future generations.'

The whole point, Alsa thought sulkily, was that she hated that and wanted it changed. They still hadn't reassured her that they could build the engine they'd promised her.

'How many is "enough"?' she asked.

'It only needs a handful,' the Eyeless said. 'One will certainly survive, there is a sixty-seven per cent chance that more than one will. The survivor or survivors will acquire the weapon.'

They'd reached a small antechamber. Through the next doorway, Alsa could see the vast interior of the inner vault, so much larger and more solid than the mental picture had made it seem.

Alsa looked over at the five Eyeless.

A handful.

The Eyeless with Jall's eyes held out its hand, waved its fingers almost cheerfully.

'A handful is six,' it told her. 'You are the sixth.'

'Touch me and I die!' the Doctor shouted.

Countless ghosts swirled away until he was out of their reach, but still they circled him. The Doctor looked ahead, then behind, but couldn't see past the ghosts. There was no way out.

One soon drifted into the eye of the storm, floated in front of him. A young man. It thought about reaching out, but hesitated… and was lost to the throng. As soon as its light had faded, another ghost had taken its place. It was screaming, silently, and even the Doctor flinched at the raw horror in its eyes.

'I'm sorry, I'm so sorry,' said the Doctor, trying to move out of its way, but there were ghosts in every direction. Dozens. Hundreds. Thousands. Their light, blue and pearl-grey, wasn't cast far from them. Every few seconds, a ghost or group of them would break from the pack to confront him.

He saw five ghostly children in short robes looking around. Four of them were crying, and the other was looking up, too surprised to react. The Doctor had to try something for them. He took the sonic screwdriver from his pocket. It had recharged enough for him to take some simple readings. They told him nothing, so he thought about it.

Could they really, somehow, be the lost souls of Arcopolis?

'There's nothing I could do,' the Doctor said quietly. 'Nothing I can do.'

Two ghosts appeared in the children's place – a man and a woman with almost angelic expressions, holding hands, trembling a little. They had gone almost as soon as they'd arrived.

'I said I'm sorry. I meant it. I'm sorry.'

Dark thoughts swirled inside the Doctor, almost filling him, almost dragging him under. All the other ghosts, his own ghosts.

'There is nothing I can do!' he whispered.

Would he have to look all 200 million of them in the eye? The Doctor vowed to do that, if that was what it took. He would stand here, tell each of them to their face, however long that took.

'Really. There's nothing.'

But he would be telling them all the same thing.

They were crowding a little closer, now, although there was still a sense of respectful distance. He had to get to the weapon. As the Doctor stepped forward, the ghosts moved with him, blocked his way.

'Can't you hear me? Don't you understand?'

There was no individual response from them, nothing to suggest a connection or a meaningful communication. There was just their shock and loss and emptiness. A hollow, objectless, grief. The sense of loss, the sense of futility, the sense of fate. It echoed within the Doctor. The sense that this shouldn't have happened, eliding without difficulty into a sense of helplessness.

'I wish I could. I wish I could do everything. I wish I could save everyone. I can't.'

Fifteen years ago, this had just been a normal world. These people hadn't been criminals or vicious or even the tiniest bit selfish. They didn't deserve this. They had been peaceful and prosperous. Charity was easily given when there was plenty for everyone, and their magnificent city was a monument that there once had been. But even now, even after all this time and hardship, the survivors of this fallen civilisation had fed him from their own meagre supplies. Everyone would have a little less to eat, but the Doctor had just sat there and slurped up their soup and chomped away on their fruit. They'd shared their lives with him, showed him kindness. Not threatened him with violence or even with confinement. They were good people. It wasn't fair. It wasn't fair on them. None of it.

What had he done for them? What could he do for them?

He checked the sonic screwdriver again.

'You're not even a blip on the sonic,' the Doctor said. 'I don't have the answers. I don't know what you are, only some of the things you're not. There's no point crowding me.'

The Doctor tried to move on, but the ghosts were consciously blocking him, now. They had become agitated.

'I mean it! Begone! Shift!'

They all moved a little closer.

'Touch me and I die. Just die. That would be it. Nothing like… what you've got. Just an end to it all. And then where would you be?'

As he'd thought that, for only a fraction of a fraction of a second, the Doctor wondered if that would be so bad.

'Do you think you're special?' the Doctor demanded.

He had seen so many people die.

'At least some of you survived,' the Doctor shouted, angry at them now. 'You weren't the *last*.'

The ghosts were all glaring, now, eyes fixed on him.

Like that pack of kids when they'd first attacked him. They weren't as angry as him. How could they be? Even all of them added together, how could they be?

'I'm the last one,' the Doctor said. 'I'm it. My people died. All of them. And Time Lords don't die just the once, you know. You have to kill us a lot more than once to make it stick.'

Still the ghosts pressed at him, some holding out their hands like beggars after a scrap of food, some shouldering towards him like they were after a fight, some apparently just wanting him to see them cry. They kept coming, like waves to a beach.

'Do you know what? In the end their sacrifice made no difference. Because *they* survived. Thousands of them, millions. Just one. It doesn't matter. It's the same thing. And… do you know what?… life is always better than death. Always. Yet I want all of *them* dead. Every single last one of them. When did I become someone who wanted to exterminate? When was that? When did they win?'

The ghosts weren't listening.

The Doctor lunged at the next one with the sonic screwdriver, brandishing it like a dagger.

'Just leave me alone!' he shouted.

And they did.

'You need to take control of your physical responses,' the Eyeless advised Alsa.

She was sobbing.

'You are more than a child, now,' the Eyeless assured her.

The five Eyeless had taken up their positions, facing the first metal gantry, standing two by two, with Alsa in the middle row. They had been sifting through her memories, acquiring her acrobatic skills, earned over years of making her way around the collapsed city. They already had similar abilities, learned from creatures called 'monkeys' they'd encountered on another planet, and they gave Alsa those to augment her own talents.

She could see the weapon chamber. One of the automatic gun turrets was there, not quite facing them.

'If we went really slowly...' she started to say. That had worked the first evening with the Doctor. The guns were, what had he called it?

'Motion sensitive,' came the voice in her head. 'That was before, when the Fortress was merely on standby.'

Weren't there other Eyeless? Why did she have to do this?

'They are on the way, but we need to act now, before the Doctor acquires the weapon.'

This was all the Doctor's fault, Alsa thought. All of it.

The Eyeless at her side was the one with green eyes.

'I'm scared,' Alsa admittedly quietly.

'Yes. Your fear is exhilarating. Inspiring. I believe I actually feel it, rather than experiencing it second hand, as is usually the case.'

The Eyeless were poised to go.

'Assemble your last thoughts,' the Eyeless said. 'If you do not survive, at least those thoughts will.'

They were waiting for the prompt. This was it... she was going to be dead in just a few minutes.

'No,' Alsa said.

The Eyeless turned its head. 'Explain.'

'It means no.'

'Our impression was that you wanted to be part of our project. That you only wanted to be more like us.'

She thought about it. She wasn't like them. Couldn't be.

'We have the ability to psychograft you permanently to a body like this one.' It raised a hand to its glass chest.

'No,' Alsa said.

She turned, could literally see the Eyeless thinking about grabbing her.

'No,' she repeated. 'This isn't right. It isn't human. This isn't how things should be. I thought you aliens would have the answers. But you don't, do you? Not you, not the Doctor.'

'With only five of us, acquiring the weapon is not assured,' the Eyeless told her.

'That's your problem,' Alsa called back, already almost back around the corner.

The Eyeless watched her go. The others were babbling at it, demanding to know whether they were going to abort the mission. The Eyeless felt another surge of anger, this time coming entirely from within itself.

'Charge,' it told them.

THIRTEEN

Defending against the alien assault on the weapon chamber was complicated by the loss of a number of perimeter turrets. Although there were only five aliens, their attack was cleverly choreographed, involving a sequence of precisely timed leaps down walkway levels. The Fortress alighted on the same sums the Eyeless had, and realised that as things stood there was a good chance one of this group was going to survive.

The surviving gun covering that section was already powered up. Now it fired, picking off an attacker. It was a test shot. The strategy computer had been concerned the refractive material the Eyeless were made of could be resistant to attack from energy weapons. It wasn't, and the Eyeless burst into fragments when the bolt hit it. One subsystem counted and tracked all the pieces, just in case, but they were inert, apart from a little psychic residue.

A subroutine warned the Fortress to pay attention to the Doctor. He was a long way from the action, but had made it to the base of the central pillar and destroyed two missiles. The column was a sheer surface, with no handholds. The Doctor was many minutes away from the weapon chamber.

The gun guarding the weapon chamber fired again, another alien fell. That situation was under control.

There was still a strong possibility at least one of the Eyeless would survive.

The Fortress was programmed to anticipate any possibility.

A subsystem warned the strategy computer that it had lost track of the Doctor.

This wasn't possible.

It ruled out the Doctor's disintegration. It scanned all the places the Doctor could be, given the topography of the Fortress and that he was a humanoid pedestrian. It ruled out every teleportation and stealth technique in its databanks, even the hypothetical ones.

When all that failed to explain where the Doctor was, the strategy computer allocated more computing power to the problem, performed a more thorough crosscheck of its records, opened every database.

A couple of subsystems warned the strategy computer that the Doctor was falling towards the weapon chamber.

The Doctor had been on the ground level, the weapon chamber was in the mathematical centre of the chamber, many hundred of storeys above that. Things fell down, not up, so the strategy computer ignored them. When the subsystems insisted, it shut them down for repair.

There was a finite number of places the Doctor could

be, given the laws of physics.

He wasn't in any of them.

The strategy computer kept looking.

The Eyeless with green eyes stood on the walkway. Shards and splinters of clear glass littered the ground. The air sizzled where the energy bolts had just sliced through it.

This Eyeless was the only survivor. It looked down. There was a narrow crack on one side where its collarbone would have been if it had had one. It didn't hurt. There was no sign of the Doctor. There was nothing between it and the open door leading to the weapon chamber. It was three steps from the doorway, safe.

It could sense the weapon in there, a strange and terrible taste.

A brown, flapping shape swept up from under the walkway at great speed, grabbed the Eyeless, lifted it three metres into the air. It was the Doctor, falling upwards, using the weight of the Eyeless to slow his ascent. But he had too much momentum, and now both of them were dropping up.

The Doctor was fiddling with something he was holding, and they both drifted back down to the walkway. The Eyeless landed on its feet, the Doctor on his side, rolling a little way towards the door before coming to a halt.

The Eyeless was between the Doctor and the door, but it didn't want to turn its back on him.

The Doctor was on his knees, pulling himself to his feet. Once he was standing, the Doctor held out his hand. A small metal cube was hovering in his palm.

'Antigravity generator,' he explained. The Eyeless could not read his mind or feelings, but the Doctor's body language and manner of speech indicated tiredness. Unlike an Eyeless, humanoid bodies grew weary. 'Used it to fall all the way from the ground. Was part of a missile that I—'

The Eyeless shoved into him, tried to push him off the walkway.

'Hey,' the Doctor said, twisting around, trying to maintain a foothold.

The Eyeless slammed into him again, but this time the Doctor was ready, and sidestepped. The Eyeless was able to right itself before its momentum could carry it over the edge or into the field of fire of any of the turrets.

Without any hesitation, the Eyeless swung for the Doctor again. The Doctor made only a half-hearted attempt to block the arm, but managed to deflect the blow.

The Eyeless adjusted its fighting style to a more informal one, elbowed the Doctor in the face, gave him a kick in the stomach and quick left-right punches to the head. A head butt after that, and the Doctor sank to his knees.

'Turns out I'm the one with a glass jaw,' the Doctor coughed.

The Eyeless moved in for the kill.

'Wait,' the Doctor said, holding a splayed hand up, almost losing his balance. 'Hang on. Don't.'

The Doctor pulled himself upright, using the Eyeless for balance.

The Eyeless recognised the expression on the Doctor's face as it drew level with its own. Alsa wore that expression. Defiance. Eyes wide with a sense of victory.

This was incompatible with the Eyeless' understanding of the situation. The Doctor had clearly made a move.

As the Doctor stepped away, the Eyeless became aware that there was a new object embedded in it. The Doctor had pushed the cube he'd been carrying into the flaw in the Eyeless' collar.

The Eyeless looked at his opponent, and saw the Doctor had his sonic screwdriver in his hand.

There was a flare of blue light, an ultrasonic squeal, and the antigravity cube activated. The Doctor, the walkway and the weapon chamber fell away from the Eyeless' feet. As it plunged skywards, it could just make out the Doctor stepping through the door into the weapon chamber.

All around the Eyeless, turrets and gun barrels twitched and took aim as it plummeted up to the apex of the inner vault, far above.

The Doctor stepped into a room that was a tiny hollow pyramid, its interior virtually featureless. There was barely room for him, let alone anyone else. Not enough room to swing an Eyeless.

He was worn out, but he had work to do and he'd already got his glasses on. He knelt in the centre of the room, concentrating on the weapon. It was suspended in a web of power lines. To human eyes, it must have looked rather plain. It was a cylinder, about a metre long, ten centimetres wide. It was burnished metal. No obvious controls or trigger, no letters or numbers or symbols. More interesting things were going on in the higher, lower and sideways dimensions, obviously.

'Infinite menace and a slight hum,' said the Doctor out loud, quoting Douglas Adams.

It was activated by touch, so he couldn't use bare hands. The Doctor fished around in Alsa's bag and found a pair of woolly gloves. He slipped one on.

He could have reached out already, plucked the weapon from its cradle. There wasn't anything stopping him. There wasn't a booby trap on the weapon – that would risk damaging it. The Doctor's hand was at his side.

Why hadn't he destroyed it already?

He knew he was holding back. He wasn't sure why. He looked around, sheepishly.

The weapon continued to hang there.

Go on, he willed himself.

It would be so easy to imagine that his hesitation was the result of some last line of defence, that it was the weapon itself staying his hand with some sort of hypnotic command. That wasn't what was happening.

The Doctor hadn't moved for over a minute, now.

He could feel the energy crackling inside the cylinder, like a trapped, perpetual lightning bolt, but perfectly black. So dark it would blind anyone who looked straight at it.

Why hadn't he destroyed it?

'We're both the last of our kind,' he concluded, quietly.

It was complex, uniquely so, but there was no mind in there, no consciousness, no life, nothing that could answer back.

Destroy it. The Eyeless could be here any minute. Destroy it.

'If the Eyeless got hold of you, then… well, that would be terrible. Worse.'

He wasn't like the Eyeless. Not at all. He travelled the universe like them, true. Flitted from planet to planet. Revelled in new experiences. Didn't put down roots. They were irresponsible, though. Not that he was the most responsible person in the universe, but his hearts were in the right places. He didn't kill people.

The Eyeless he'd just sent plummeting up to its doom might have been the last one.

The memory of a reptile hand clawing at soot-stained limestone. The Doctor's thoughts had returned to the battle with the dinosaur man in the clock tower of the Houses of Parliament, the Steggosian he'd told Gar and Alsa about. The Doctor could recall the creature's rank, not his name. There was no one left now who could remind him. The Doctor had let the Steggosian Captain fall to his death, knowing he was the last of his kind.

He remembered the last of the Racnoss, consumed in flames. He remembered the death throes of the Pyroviles. He remembered an army of Daleks sucked into the howling Void. He remembered Richard Lazarus, dying in a blitzkrieg of sound courtesy of a cathedral organ and the sonic screwdriver.

They weren't *victims*. They had been poised to kill, springing traps they'd set themselves. The best word to describe them was *monsters*, and the best thing to do with monsters was fight them.

The people of Arcopolis, they were victims.

What if the weapon could be used for good?

The Doctor hadn't taken his eyes off it.

'There's no such thing as evil science,' he said finally.

'Anything can be turned into a weapon. Anything. If you worried about what wicked men might do, you'd never invent anything. You'd never light a fire or pick up a rock. You can kill people with medicine, drown them in a bucket of spring water, burn them up in sunshine.'

The opposite was true, too: any sword could be beaten into a ploughshare, every spear into a pruning hook. It was sometimes difficult to see how. He, alone in all the universe, had the knowledge to do it with this weapon. No one else understood the science like he did. More than that, he knew it was at least possible, because he'd seen the ghosts. The weapon wasn't meant to leave traces, but the ghosts were traces.

There's more to this weapon than I thought.

The Doctor tapped his teeth with his fingers, then rapped his forehead with his knuckles. This was a change of plan, no doubt about it. He could study the weapon, learn a bit more about it. It might not be possible. There was a chance, though.

If I destroyed the weapon now, I would lose that chance for ever.

'Good point,' the Doctor noted.

He peered up at the weapon over the top of his glasses. He might be able to use it to create, not destroy. Reverse its polarity, or whatever.

Every instinct was telling him to destroy it.

He took a step back, thought for a moment. Was it possible to use this for the good?

No one else possibly could. You might.

The Doctor decided not to destroy the weapon.

Some superstitious urge made the thought of touching

it uncomfortable, even through a glove. He slipped Alsa's bag off his shoulder, turned it inside out and put his hands in, like it was a giant oven mitten, then reached into the web of power lines and began plucking the weapon from it. The cylinder was solid, surprisingly heavy. It was warm, even through the artificial fibre of the bag. The detached cables still buzzed, still had enough energy in them to bite.

The Doctor was cradling the weapon now, needed both hands to lift it.

One last power line to detach, then the weapon would be free, and he would turn the bag back outside in and hide it out of sight and out of mind. As the Doctor tugged it loose, there was a clattering noise from outside the chamber. He glanced through the door.

The very last thing he saw before the whole Fortress went dark was an army of Eyeless charging down the walkway towards him, arms raised like clubs.

There was a theory that the way to defeat an enemy was to turn their own strength against them.

'Well,' the Doctor sniffed, 'at least I have plenty to work with.'

The Fortress strategy computer recognised that it was about to be deactivated, knew it had no options remaining. It drew all its strength from the weapon, and the Doctor was well on the way to disconnecting it.

A thousand subroutines had warned it not to underestimate the Doctor from the moment he'd been identified, yet it had done just that.

It had just been overrun. Eighty-eight of the aliens inside it, all exploiting the safe route to the weapon chamber, all heading for the Doctor. The guns in that section had all been disabled, and the power would be shut off within moments.

The Doctor would destroy the aliens, of course. The strategy he would adopt was straightforward. The computer felt no regret or anger. It cycled through its complete list of strategies one last time, not knowing anything else to do.

And then the machine stopped.

When the lights had gone out, the Eyeless leading the charge had been within seconds of reaching the weapon chamber.

Now it was pitch black but, as if to compensate, the air was saturated with sound. The noise was made up of almost a couple of hundred heavy glass footfalls on metal, echoing off the walls.

Instantly the command went out, and the Eyeless came to a halt. Had a squad of human soldiers tried to do the same, the line would have concertinaed and slipped up; maybe a couple of people would even have been pushed or tripped over the edge of the narrow walkway. Their telepathy allowed the Eyeless to coordinate the move.

The immediate situation was easy enough to comprehend, and broke like a wave over the Eyeless: the Doctor was in the weapon chamber, dead ahead of them. Through the one doorway leading into the chamber, they'd seen the Doctor with the weapon in his hand. With the power offline, that meant there were no active defence systems.

They had to get to the weapon, and quickly.

As the echoes died down, they shared their memories and impressions of the inside of the Fortress, swiftly overlaying them all, self-correcting the discrepancies, until they had built up a mental map of the structure. This was a rare process for them, to so totally give up their individuality. They elided their memories and perceptions, effortlessly becoming, to all practical purposes, a single creature, a beast with 88 heads, 176 legs, 1,056 fingers, one mind and one objective:

Kill the Doctor.

He couldn't disguise the sounds of his feet scuffing the floor, his breathing, his double heartbeat. Eighty-eight of them heard him at the doorway.

As one, they charged at him.

The foremost reached the doorway and the Doctor wasn't there. Three of them felt their way into the chamber. They held their hands out, thirty-six fingers twitching like antennae.

One of the Eyeless brushed against a power line, which sparked and froze it rigid, forcing another one to step aside, into the path of another power line. Another spark. The third was trapped between them.

The three of them would recover in minutes. The remaining eighty-five knew that the Doctor was no longer in the weapon chamber. He couldn't be far.

One of the Eyeless, towards the middle of the pack, was shoved aside, toppled over the edge. Two of its comrades managed to grab it before it was lost for ever. The one nearest those two swiped out to grab the Doctor, who must have been responsible for the initial shove. Instead, it grabbed one of the rescuers, unbalanced it. All four tipped over, off into the darkness.

Sharing this sensation, all the Eyeless reeled, moved to brace for when they landed.

Eighty-one flares of blue light; eighty-one electronic squeals; eighty-one Doctors, holding eighty-one sonic screwdrivers aloft, eighty-one ultimate weapons tucked under eighty-one arms. The Eyeless lurched in eighty-one different directions to grab him.

The Eyeless reeled, assimilated the experience. There was only one Doctor, but all of them had seen him then sent the information to the others.

Simultaneously, they felt the rush of air from above.

There was a grinding crash, followed by a series of creaks. The ranks of the Eyeless had been diminished, bisected.

Sixteen Eyeless leapt out the way, finding either air under their feet, or the side of a comrade, bumping them until they were over the edge of the walkway. The Eyeless felt the air whistling past them, felt the impacts. Most were able to swing an arm out, connect with some cable or other walkway.

Nineteen other Eyeless had just vanished.

The wave of realisation broke over the survivors – the blue light hadn't just been to disorientate them, it had loosened a large section of pipeline that had been hanging overhead.

That pipe was now a curved wall dividing the Eyeless into two small groups – one of seventeen individuals and one of twenty-nine.

There was a creak and the wall moved.

'Ah…' the Doctor's voice called out, from just above all forty-six of the Eyeless.

Another creak.

'Look,' the voice continued. 'Um… you have lights in your hands, remember? Might be an idea to use them.'

They remembered. Three of them raised their hands and activated them. Three soft golden lanterns in the darkness.

The Doctor was standing on top of a cross-section of fallen pipe that had landed square in the middle of the walkway. It was about the same height as the Eyeless.

The Doctor silently surveyed the scene, then started running backwards on the spot, and the pipe started rolling towards the exit.

The twenty-nine Eyeless on that side started running ahead of it – rather that than leaping off or being crushed. None of them had time to note the gleeful glint in the Doctor's eye. He had only got the pipe a little way, though, before the Eyeless behind him worked out that they could shove at it, trying to steer it.

All this activity meant that the lanterns went out again. The sound of the pipe creaking and rolling along filled the darkness.

After a few moments, there was a great clang as the pipe crashed into the outer wall of the vault. It was wedged in place.

The Eyeless in front of the pipe were blocked out of the inner vault, for the moment at least. The Doctor was also boxed in, though.

The Eyeless prepared to go in for the kill, three climbing up onto the top of the pipe with the help of the others.

The Doctor wasn't there.

Moments after the lanterns had gone out, the Doctor had grabbed a dangling piece of cable and clambered up it. The Eyeless had been too busy pushing the pipe to notice, and the racket that it had made covered his tracks.

He'd climbed up a couple of levels and found a narrow gantry, all of this in the dark, every handhold and escape route found by blindly flailing an arm.

He was three or four levels higher, now. He flopped down on the solid platform, needing to get his breath back. He tried not to make any noise.

The weapon was still in the bag, weighing on his mind. He felt exhilarated, full of possibilities. He could hear the Eyeless clattering around below him, caught glimpses of them moving, arms aloft and glowing, hurrying along the tops of gantries and the thickest pipelines like palace guards. They were all many levels below him. The search pattern wasn't as systematic and ordered as he'd expected from them. He had them rattled.

The Eyeless were still angry and agitated, like they had been infected. They'd been changed by their experiences here. Ideas, attitudes, beliefs, emotions… they could rapidly spread through any society. Jokes or pop tunes or new slang or catchphrases could appear one day and everyone in a country would know them within a week or two. The Doctor had met hiveminded races before. They all had a slightly different mechanism for spreading the word, but their great strength was that they could share information instantly and totally efficiently.

These Eyeless were addicted to anger now, took pleasure from it. If they got into contact with the rest of their kind, the anger would spread, across the galaxy. An advanced race with a massive space navy, an urge to steal, fuelled by anger. They'd swarm across the cosmos.

It wasn't as though the universe was short of monsters already. He'd have to nip them in the bud.

The Doctor glanced down at Alsa's bag.

There was an easy way to do this. A surgical strike. Use the weapon. Just once.

Exterminate.

The Doctor shivered, physically pulled himself back from the bag.

Destroying the Eyeless because of what they *might* become? All so easy, using the weapon.

The simplest thing was just to destroy it. Here and now.

He stood, stiffly, but also a little wobbly on his feet. Not a brilliant combination when the way around here was across narrow gantries and on top of pipelines.

The Doctor could have used Alsa's torch, but the Eyeless would be on him like... he was going to say like moths to a flame, but moths tended to lose that battle.

He'd be safe in the dark for a little while.

There was a light forming in front of him.

This was really bad timing, he thought, tucking himself out of sight.

The ghost of a very, very old woman, looking around, perplexed. She didn't see the Doctor. Lit from within, the lines and wrinkles of her face were stark, spidery.

The Doctor looked down. He could see Eyeless looking up, calculating a route to the ghost. Then, like a dying ember, the ghost just faded away.

The Fortress was without power, now. The ghosts weren't a defence system, after all. That nagged at the Doctor. So what *were* they?

They weren't a coincidence.

It would be almost comforting to think that they were the restless souls of the 200 million killed here in Arcopolis, that the injustice of their deaths had scarred the very atoms and molecules. Nature had laws, but no justice. If there was a ghost for every untimely death, there would be few places in the universe that weren't haunted.

The weapon had done this. It was a logic puzzle, but the answer wasn't in the programming of the Fortress, it was somewhere in the laws of physics. When a ghost touched someone, they both vanished – that was part of the puzzle, too.

He had to get out of the Fortress to somewhere safer, somewhere away from the glass men and the ghosts themselves.

The Doctor lowered himself down a level, scurried on his hands and knees through a narrow crawlspace. Fifty metres of that, and he found an access hatch that he slid open. He climbed out onto what the acoustics told him was a wide platform, dusted himself off, slung the bag over his shoulder, turned and almost walked straight into a ghost.

This was a ghost he'd already met. Behind it, other ghosts, dozens of them and more all the time. They cast light and shadows over the platform.

Last time, they'd communicated via Alsa's comm, which was gone now. The Doctor remembered the idea he'd had for talking to the Eyeless. He slipped a slim leather wallet from his pocket, and opened up the psychic paper.

'You can hear me,' he whispered. 'I can't hear you. Here, let's try this.'

The ghost nodded, relieved, and tiny, neat copperplate handwriting appeared on the paper.

I am Gyll.

'Yes, I... recognise you. Don't you recognise me?' The Doctor found himself wondering if this was how Gyll's handwriting had always looked. With all their computers and robots, would the people of Arcopolis have even bothered learning to use pens?

I'm not sure. Something is different.

'Yes.'

The Doctor opened the bag, let the ghost see inside it.

'This is the weapon that killed you,' the Doctor said. 'This is what murdered you all. Don't touch it.'

The ghost drifted towards it, head turning to get a better look. And, as it looked down, and he saw it alongside the weapon for the first time, it came to the Doctor what the ghosts were.

So small a thing.

'Yes,' he said quietly.

Now you have it.

'I've promised to destroy it, the very first moment I can.'

Yes, I know you mean to do that.

'I have to break another promise. I can't save you.'

The ghost stared at him, blankly.

'I can't save you, because I know what you are, now,' the Doctor said. 'You're not Gyll, not really.'

I am Gyll.

'No. The weapon killed Gyll. Killed everyone. But you can't destroy matter and energy so utterly. It's impossible. There's always something left behind. Even if you drop a nuclear bomb, you burn shadows into the concrete and tarmac. Blast shadows, they're called.'

The Doctor paused, took the time to breathe in.

'Gyll was ripped from the universe, but the imprint remained. You're a blast shadow. A complicated one, because Gyll was killed by this very, very complicated weapon. But you're only the echo of the ghost of consciousness. Here.'

He let the equations flow from his mind and across the psychic paper, a model of eleven-dimensional time and space. Beautiful, beautiful mathematics.

I don't understand that.

'You don't have to. All that you need to know is that I do understand it. You're a shadow, and the person that cast it is long gone.'

I am Gyll.

'No,' the Doctor said simply.

I know I am.

'No. You ghosts aren't real, you're holes in reality. Anyone you touch falls right out of the universe.'

Something was agitating the ghosts behind the Doctor, making them flit over and around him. They couldn't have overheard what he'd said. Were they moving to block his escape?

They weren't… They were looking at something ahead of him. The sea of ghosts parted just long enough for the Doctor to see a small army of glass men walking slowly towards him.

At their head was the one with Jall's eyes. It had a charred pit the size of a fist in its chest. A dozen paces from the Doctor, though, it came to a halt, as did all the Eyeless behind it.

What is happening?

'You're holding them in place,' the Doctor reasoned. 'They are powerful psychics. So many ghosts, all those memories, all that pain and anguish. It's paralysing them. Like a deafening sound would stop a person in their tracks.'

The one in front tries to communicate. It is so angry.

'What is it saying?'

That you want the weapon for yourself, that they are the Eyeless & want only to study it. That they had nothing to do with the death of Arcopolis.

'It calls itself an Eyeless, but it has eyes,' the Doctor noted.

The ghost moved forward, as did a number of the others. They all peered into the glass head, saw the two eyeballs mounted there. The Eyeless squirmed under the scrutiny, but couldn't retreat. It was like its feet had been glued to the metal floor. The ghosts looked around at each other, puzzled, then all but one of them fell back.

'Human eyes,' the Doctor confirmed. 'Ask it to explain.'

The ghost just swept over to the Eyeless, who writhed, tried to escape, but couldn't. The ghost calmly took its memories. The ghost floated in front of the Eyeless for a few seconds, like an attentive listener.

'Those are Jall's eyes it's wearing,' the Doctor said quietly. 'Ask it who Jall is.'

The ghost turned back, stared into the bright green eyeballs, looked back at the Doctor, shocked. It was remembering it all, taking the thoughts and memories from the Eyeless. Seeing what the Doctor couldn't – the moment of Jall's death, the drinking in of her last, terrified thoughts, the taking of the eyes.

Finally, words appeared on the psychic paper.

Dela had a daughter?

'Yes.'

We only talked about children.

The ghost didn't seem to know if it had heard good news or not. It had no memories of the last fifteen years, just a snapshot of Gyll's mind at the moment of death.

'Things are different now. Everything has changed. Dela has many children. The only way for the people of Arcopolis to survive. Jall was the eldest.'

& now Dela's firstborn is dead.

'Dela is alive,' the Doctor told the ghost. 'She should be safe, but thanks to this creature I can't be sure of that.

I made a promise to Dela. You can help me keep it. But... there's a cost.'

The ghost held out a finger, almost touched the Doctor's lips. There was no need to say more.

Then it fell onto the Eyeless, hands thrust out like talons, thrusting its elbows deep into the glass chest. The ghost was silently screaming, swirling through the body and mind of the Eyeless. The other glass men were powerless to move, let alone defend their colleague. The one with Jall's eyes managed to lift one foot, at last, but it lost its balance, had to send its hand to the edge of the platform to keep itself from falling over the edge.

Its glass was losing its brilliance and looked almost charred. The Eyeless raised its right hand, trying to use the weapon embedded there, but couldn't summon any light.

A second ghost hurtled past the Doctor and through another of the Eyeless. Then another, then another, then another. All of them, throwing themselves into the Eyeless ranks, tearing the strength of the glass men out with their bare hands.

The Eyeless swatted at them, not connecting with anything. The ghosts were dashed to pieces as they hit the Eyeless, vanishing when they touched anyone, as they had before, but they eroded their opponents in turn. This was an entirely silent process and as each ghost dissipated, their light faded, and the interior of the Fortress grew a little darker.

'An eye for an eye,' the Doctor said, so softly the words were almost drowned out by the sound of shattering glass.

He had seen enough death, and gained no satisfaction from the thought of more. Wearily, he watched, waited until the inevitable moment when the last light faded.

Kill you.

The words crashed through the Doctor's mental defences.

The ghosts had gone, but one Eyeless was still there, the sheen of its skin faded, pitted. Damaged by contact with the ghosts, but surviving through sheer force of will. The glass man rose to its knees, watery, broken light seeping from its damaged right hand. Of course it was the one with Jall's eyes. The last of the Eyeless.

Its face was level with the Doctor's. They were inches apart, at most.

Kill you.

It was the Doctor's own voice. He was the bringer of darkness, the oncoming storm, the murderer of whole worlds.

The Doctor couldn't tell if he was thinking that or the Eyeless was thinking it for him. He found he wasn't resisting as the Eyeless' hands closed around his neck, as he began sinking to his knees. The fight had gone from him. This was his death, and there was no one in this universe who would mourn him, and the Eyeless would take the weapon.

Unless.

'I have something for you,' he managed to croak out.

The Eyeless stood motionless.

'You can't have the weapon,' the Doctor said, getting to his feet. He held out a small metal shape on a loop of chain.

'You like trading? You always want something new? How about this key?'

The Eyeless looked warily at it.

'The key to my TARDIS,' the Doctor said. 'You were right. That blue box is a time machine. But you've not been able to get inside, have you? I… will do you a deal.'

The Doctor looked down at the pieces of glass scattered on the gantry.

'You ran the numbers,' he said quietly. 'Well… run these numbers: if you let me live and let me destroy the weapon, you can have my TARDIS.'

The Eyeless took a step forward, reached out, but the Doctor snatched the key away.

'The most important thing is destroying the weapon,' the Doctor said quietly, almost to himself. 'No one should have it. Not me, not you, no one. I will pay any price to see that weapon broken in half.'

The key dangled tantalisingly out of the reach of the Eyeless.

'I know what you're thinking,' the Doctor said. 'You could kill me, take the key, take the weapon.'

The Eyeless was careful not to betray its reaction.

'The TARDIS won't let you in unless I tell it to. After that, it's simple enough. The flight computer is, well, let's just say it's fairly intuitive. This isn't a trick… well, I would say that. Honest, it's not a trick. Trust me, I'm a doctor. But this is the deal: you watch me destroy the weapon, I give you the key. I'll just stay here, with the villagers. Live out my life. Look after them, if they'll have me.'

The Doctor paused, sagged a little.

'I can do good here. You get a time machine and you can fly off in it. Hand on hearts, right now I can't imagine you'd do any more harm than I've already done.'

He looked straight at the Eyeless, a glint in his eye.

'You're a strategist, you're a rational being. It's a good deal. Particularly for you... individually.'

The Eyeless turned its head slightly.

'Nothing wrong with a bit of ambition,' the Doctor assured it, raising an eyebrow. 'Eh? Know what I mean?'

The Eyeless held out its hand.

'Say no more,' the Doctor said.

The Eyeless blocked his way. It held out its left hand, palm up.

'You can't have it yet. Let's go outside, then I'll destroy the weapon.'

It stayed where it was, twitched its fingers.

The Doctor strained to look around it, both sides. 'Oh... all right.'

Its glass wrist had begun to ripple, eager for the trophy.

'Handy,' said the Doctor, his mouth managing to flicker at the pun. 'You'll never lose the key this way. And, of course, if you're... stuck with the key, you, uniquely among all the Eyeless, get to be the TARDIS captain. Primus inter pares, eh? If you'll pardon my Welsh.'

The Eyeless looked down at the TARDIS key. The possibilities started to surge through its mind. It leapt for the Doctor, greedily gripping the lapels of the Doctor's coat with a six-fingered hand, the Eyeless' mind grabbing for the Doctor's mind.

There was something he wasn't saying, wasn't there?

His secret. That it was the Doctor who—

'Oh, shut it,' the Doctor snapped, shrugging off the grip of the glass hands. The psychic onslaught continued and for a moment, they were eye to eye. The bright green, unblinking, stolen eyes. The Doctor and the Eyeless both understood what had to happen next, and that it would soon all be over.

'You're a thief,' the Doctor said softly, his mouth close to the side of the Eyeless' head. 'A murderer. And I meant everything I said, and you had your chance and you blew it.'

The Eyeless thrust its hand into the bag to grab the weapon. The Doctor threw his hand out to stop him.

A hand brushed against the weapon, grabbed it.

The weapon fired.

A moment later, the Doctor was alone in the darkness.

FOURTEEN

He strode from the wreckage. He emerged from the great gash in the side of the dead Fortress, into the sunlit Car Factory. The weapon was still in the bag slung over his shoulder. Rubble and smashed glass and bits of rag were strewn over the factory floor. Great chunks and beams of the concrete ceiling had come down.

The silence pressed against his eardrums.

He'd survived. At least he assumed he had. Perhaps, like Gyll, he only thought he'd survived. He didn't know exactly what the weapon had done. Why it had spared him. He didn't know if it had spared anyone else.

He might truly be alone, now.

He needed to get back to the TARDIS. He turned, wanting companionship, more than anything, but there was no one beside him.

It was a warm afternoon, so he took off his coat and folded it over his arm and Alsa's bag and what was inside the bag. He could feel the sun against his face, at least.

He must be alive.

He had scoured the darkness. The instant the weapon had been activated, the Eyeless had gone. He had been the only thing left in there, the only trace of life.

There had been no light, no sound, the air had been perfectly still. All there had been was the metallic smell, faintly like dried blood, and the press of his feet through the soles of his trainers down onto the platform, and the throb of the bruise on his temple. Without those, it would have been oblivion, nothing. He had felt numb, dissociated. It had crossed his mind that he was imagining everything, merely remembering. Then he had understood: if he could have those thoughts, he still existed.

He thought, therefore he was.

Now, outside, sunlight and silence streaming over him, he sat on a metal block. He ached all over. Behind him, the Fortress was creaking, cracking.

He thought of the weapon destroying all life. Not just the Eyeless, but all the humans here, all the trees and other plants and bacteria, then out into the universe, its fingers poking into the gaps between space and time and rooting out every life form on every world and between all the worlds, striking so swiftly no one could even see it as it went about its work.

Everyone dead. Everyone dead but him.

Had that happened? How long would he be left travelling on his own? How long would he need to accept there was no one else? How many dead planets would he have to visit?

The rubble that had tumbled down had blocked every way out but one. One of the vast machines – the sonic screwdriver the size of a car wash – hadn't buckled. Its arch now formed a short tunnel, the one way out of here.

It also gave him something to do. He found the control panel for the machine, which was on the side facing the Fortress. He brushed off the dust and fragments from it. The device was fully charged. It absorbed sound, and there would have been plenty when the floors above it collapsed.

He whispered things to the machine, told it some of his fears and secrets.

'Doctor!' a voice called.

It was Dela. She ran over to him, through the arch and to the other side, and was rather surprised when he grabbed her, pulled her off her feet and gave her such a hug she almost snapped in two.

'Bad day?' she asked, when he finally let go.

'Oh, you know… I stole an infinitely powerful super-weapon, exchanged text messages with the dead, had an ethics debate with a psychotic teenage girl and a fight in pitch blackness with an army of glass men. An average sort of Saturday, really. It's still Saturday, isn't it?'

'I think it's still Saturday morning. Are… are you all right?'

'The Eyeless that killed Jall is dead.'

'The one with her eyes?'

'Yeah.'

'Thank you.'

He nodded. 'They're all dead.'

And eventually Dela said it was probably for the best.

'And the weapon?' she asked.

Hesitation.

'Doctor?'

'The Eyeless didn't get their hands on it,' he told her. 'It's in the bag.'

The bag was draped over his shoulder.

'The joke is… the joke is that it didn't work. Twice, now, the weapon has failed to do what it was designed to do.'

'This is what it does when it fires a dud?'

'Yes.'

They sat in silence for a little longer.

'I miss—' Dela said.

'I thought—' he said at the same time, then, 'Go on.'

'No, you first.'

'I thought it might have destroyed everything.'

'Everyone but you.'

'Everyone but me.'

'The weapon could really do that?'

'Yes.'

'We still might be the last two people.'

'Yes. What were you going to say just now?'

'What? Oh… I miss the birdsong,' she said. 'Sorry, I don't have the grand thoughts you have.'

The Doctor broke into his first grin since emerging from the Fortress.

'Why haven't you destroyed the weapon?' she asked.

'I will… I will now,' the Doctor agreed. 'Right now.'

The pair of them stood, helping each other up.

'Well,' said the Doctor, then seeing Dela's expression, 'Um, why are you looking at me like—?'

A waft of perfume and the bag was tugged hard off his shoulder.

The Doctor turned to see Alsa, a wild sneer on her face, her nose caked in dried blood. He ducked out of the way as she swung the bag at him. No, not at him – at Dela. The metal cylinder inside the bag connected with the side of Dela's head, and she slumped.

'It's quite effective at close range, yeah?' Alsa noted.

Alsa had felt the Eyeless die through their own senses. Those that had been gunned down, those in the ships, they'd just faded away. They had never meant anything to her… but when the one with green eyes went, there was a moment when Alsa thought she'd also become nothing.

As soon as she'd seen the archway, she knew the Doctor would have to come out this way. She'd waited, kept out of sight as Dela had gone past. As soon as she saw the Doctor leave the Fortress, she'd just known the weapon was in the bag. *Her* bag. She had no idea how – it wasn't just because there weren't many other places it could be, she really could sense it.

This had been her plan right from the first moment she'd heard about the weapon, realised what it could do: let the Doctor get it, force him to give it to her. Alsa stepped back into the arch, blocked the only way out. The thing in the bag was twice as heavy as she'd been expecting. She couldn't look at it yet, couldn't take her eyes off the Doctor, needed to keep both her hands free.

'You killed the Eyeless.'

'Yes.'

'All of them?'

'Here, yes. Beyond that, I don't know.'

She had fleeting images of other worlds, pulses of intense emotion, flakes of esoteric science and history, remembered what it had been like to briefly *be* an Eyeless. Was that memory all that was left of them?

'Alsa, that Eyeless had started to infect the others. It couldn't see any further than itself. It thought its problems were the universe's. And you think the same, don't you?'

'But it's OK, because I'm just a kid? Go on then – push off. Leave me to it. You're not going to solve anything.'

'Your civilisation will survive. It will take time, many generations, before it thrives. But it will survive.'

'I saw a way out of this.'

Alsa hefted the bag, and she saw the Doctor flinch.

'It would mean even more death. Everything touched by that weapon becomes corrupted.'

'I thought that you were our saviour. I thought you could change things. I thought the Eyeless would.'

'I know,' the Doctor said, not taking his eyes off her. 'And I'm sorry you thought that.'

'All I wanted was to be treated the same as an adult.'

'Oh... you really don't want me to do that,' he told her darkly.

'I've never wanted anything else from anyone!' Alsa shouted, holding up the bag. 'I just want someone to take me seriously! If I've got to *use* this weapon to do that—'

'"Seriously"?' the Doctor said. 'Oh, I can do *seriously*.'

The Doctor held his arm out, pointed the sonic screwdriver up above her head. Alsa looked up. For the first time, she registered that this archway was part of a machine. A metal bolt above her head slid shakily back and locked into a new configuration.

The machine was humming. Blue lights started flickering all around her on the sides of the archway, in weird patterns. There were three other bolts – one on either side, one between her feet.

Alsa steadied herself, stared right at him, mouth open, eyes narrow.

'That machine is like my sonic screwdriver,' the Doctor said. 'You're standing in the resonator cage.'

Alsa shrugged, partly to look brave, partly because she didn't understand what the Doctor meant.

The Doctor pivoted his arm around, pointed it at a pile of engines. The tip of his sonic screwdriver flared and the engines just fell apart, the tiny components cascading down.

The Doctor turned to aim the sonic screwdriver back at Alsa. She didn't look up the next time he activated it. The bolt to her left slid back and locked into place, just like the first. The Doctor blinked, lowered the sonic screwdriver.

'Two more bolts to go,' she told him, feeling brave, proud of herself. She had the strength for this, she knew that.

'I think the Eyeless altered your mind,' the Doctor said.

'That would be so much easier, wouldn't it? You could kill me in good conscience, then.'

The Doctor lowered his sonic screwdriver.

'Oh I could never kill you, Alsa,' he said. His voice was tinged with sadness. 'But what about you? Could you kill? Really?'

Alsa already had one hand tugging on the bag's flap, and now she saw the weapon for the first time. It was a metal tube, that was all. It was humming to itself.

'This is it?' she asked.

It surprised Alsa how calm the Doctor looked.

'Touch it, it will activate,' he said. 'It'll kill everyone you want it to.'

She'd won. Alsa knew she'd beaten the Doctor. That's why he was so calm – he knew there was nothing else he could do. He couldn't even kill her.

Why was she hesitating? Dela was slowly coming round, shaking her head and getting unsteadily to her feet, watching Alsa warily. Was it because of Dela that she was hesitating?

The Doctor was looking right at her. 'There are no rules here, now,' he said. 'No Jennver. No monsters forcing you to do anything. No authority. No laws. No witnesses. You can do whatever you want to me. Anything you want to Dela. No one can stop you, no one can punish you afterwards.'

Alsa thought about it. It *sounded* like the ultimate freedom.

'Do it and no one will tell you off, or hold you to account.'

Alsa looked down at the weapon again. It would be so easy to shut the Doctor up. Very easy.

'You're on your own. No one but yourself to blame.'

He let that sink in.

'It's up to you. Your choice. I made my own choice just now. Will yours be any different? Do what you want.'

Alsa could feel something beneath the metal surface of the weapon, something inside it, around it, working into her like roots and damp into an old wall. She could almost feel it starting to eat away at her.

'All it does is destroy?' she asked.

'Yes.'

'This isn't a trick?'

'You know it isn't.'

'Yeah… I know.'

Alsa couldn't make herself move. Couldn't decide. She could destroy anything. *Everything*.

'It's not easy, is it?' the Doctor said.

'No.'

'The fate of all life in the universe is in your hands, Alsa. Literally in your hands.'

'This is what it's like for you all the time?'

'Oh yes,' the Doctor said quietly. 'And doesn't it just drive you mad?'

Alsa stepped off out of the arch, wrapped the bag closed and handed it to the Doctor.

'Help me,' she said.

The Doctor took the bag, weighed it in his hand. There was no relief in his eyes. Why would there be, now he had the weapon weighing him down again?

'I don't know what to do,' Alsa told him. 'I live here. I don't know anywhere but here. You could take me back.'

'Back?' Dela asked.

'His TARDIS is a time machine. He could take me back to *before*. He could take us all back.'

The Doctor was shaking his head. 'It doesn't work like that. That isn't what happened.'

He'd wrapped the bag around itself, cocooned the weapon.

'Destroy the weapon,' Dela insisted. 'You can at least do that. Do it now.'

'Yes.' The Doctor paused, looked down like that genuinely hadn't even occurred to him. 'I need to get it away from here. I have to get back to the TARDIS.'

'The Eyeless said they had taken possession of it.'

'We don't need to worry about the Eyeless any more,' the Doctor said quietly.

'Take me with you,' Alsa said.

'All right,' said the Doctor, distracted. Then he looked up sharply, realised what he'd said. Dela was staring at him, empty-eyed.

'I'll come back,' the Doctor told Dela. 'I'll…'

He paused. Looked at Alsa, then Dela, then up at what was left of the ceiling.

'Actually, yes. Come on, Alsa. I know how we do this.'

'You can help me?'

'Squaring circles. What I do best,' he declared happily. He indicated the arch to Alsa. 'Lead on, McDuck.'

'I don't understand.'

'No, you don't. Lost in translation. But you will understand. That's the point.'

'I'd better.'

'I wouldn't mind an explanation, too,' Dela said.

'All in good time,' the Doctor chuckled.

The three of them stepped through the arch. Alsa was holding Dela's hand.

After walking another twenty metres or so, the Doctor turned back. 'Hang on, I almost forgot.'

He pointed the sonic screwdriver at the archway, and the final bolts fell into place. The air filled with sound which then spiralled into the archway, building and building and compressing. Finally, the energy released in a single burst, which shot out away from them, hit the Fortress, took it to pieces.

The black metal walls slipped apart, avalanched, sploshed down into the lake far below. Each layer fell away in turn, faster and faster as the supporting structure was weakened, pieces of pipe and gantry and platform and gun turret and doors and light fittings, until the whole Fortress had gone, and there was nothing but sunlight and fresh air and the sound of tons of metal crashing into the water in its place.

Dela, Alsa and the Doctor were laughing, but couldn't hear each other. They had to clamp their hands over their ears.

FIFTEEN

The Doctor kept his promises to both Alsa and Dela. Now, a large blue wooden crate, decorated with rows of square panels and a flashing light on top, arrived in the centre of the settlement.

A messenger boy had run to Dela even before the strange noise it made had fully died down.

The Doctor stepped out of the TARDIS, looked up at the huge metal sculpture that now dominated the central square.

'That's new,' he noted.

'It's old,' Alsa told him, puzzled, stepping out after him. 'It's called *Dance of Days*. They must have moved it from the city this morning. Is this what you were going to show me?'

'No. Look around.'

There were people everywhere. All ages, plenty of kids. The distant buildings of Arcopolis were covered in ivy, most of them. Others had tarnished, become brick red. There was a gap in the skyline where the Fortress had been, like the city was missing a tooth.

A crowd was gathering around the TARDIS.

'It took us weeks to get it here,' a man said.

Alsa wouldn't have recognised him if he hadn't had his hands in his pockets. He wore a tool belt, and his hair was starting to thin a little.

'Gar?'

He nodded.

Alsa turned, drank it all in. 'This is the future.'

'Yup,' the Doctor said. He was also looking around. Everyone clearly knew who he was. Many of them had been there twenty years before. The others must have heard stories about him. An older woman stepped out from the group.

'This is your time machine?' Dela asked. Her hair was extraordinarily, vividly white, now. She looked radiant.

'Yes.'

'It doesn't look like a time machine, it looks like…' She wasn't sure what it looked like.

'There's a reason,' the Doctor assured her. 'A really good one.'

'You don't look a day older.'

'I'm not. Not quite.'

She ran a hand along his temple. 'You still have the bruise.'

'You must have scores more children by now,' the Doctor said lightly.

'Only one more. Lios. A boy. Well, a man now. It's all grandchildren these days.'

The Doctor beamed. 'Hang on. Almost forgot. Brought you a present.'

He nipped back into the TARDIS.

'And the weapon?' Dela asked.

Alsa held out a small, charred piece of metal for Dela and Gar to inspect. 'We went to an asteroid – like a little planet. It didn't have any air, so we had to wear spacesuits. There was a plasma vent, like a pit of energy. We dropped it in there and the weapon just opened up. We couldn't look at what was inside, but once it was out, it couldn't survive in our universe. Then we went to another planet and ate weird stuff called "burgers".'

The Doctor emerged from the TARDIS holding a birdcage. Inside were two birds that would have fitted in the palm of his hand. Their feathers were a rainbow, from their red caps to their violet wingtips.

'Kegronian Halcyons,' the Doctor said. 'A breeding pair. Widely regarded as having the most beautiful plumage and song of any bird in the universe. Very adaptable. Not much meat on them, but… well, that's good news for the Kegronian Halcyon, isn't it, all things considered?'

The Doctor opened a small door on the side of the cage, and the two birds pushed their way out, then spread their colourful wings and they were off, swooping around each other, darting towards the city and so many potential roosts.

The others watched the birds, but the Doctor was staring at the necklace Dela wore – a glass pendant.

She glanced over at him. 'They're all over the city, get washed up in the streams. The water wears them smooth.'

Gar was handing the Doctor one, but he held up his hand. 'Won't work on me. Alsa?'

Alsa took one. 'Oh…'

'Memories?' the Doctor asked.

'Yes,' Gar said. 'Some from the Eyeless, some from the ghosts.'

'A source of technical knowledge?'

'And a way of broadening our horizons.'

Dela smiled. 'Gyll,' she said, touching her stone. 'At least… I like to think so.'

'So you go into the City, now?' Alsa asked.

'Yes,' Dela said. 'We choose to. We have choices, now. There are so many of us, we've actually lost count. Which is silly, there aren't all that many. Thousands.'

Alsa smiled.

'It makes everything a lot easier.'

The Doctor was grinning. 'Who says there are no second chances, eh? What wally ever said that? See, Alsa, it all works out.'

'Yes…'

'So now you've seen this, I can take you back, safe in the knowledge that it all turns out for the best and—'

'Doctor,' Dela cut in, 'it didn't happen that way.'

'It doesn't what?'

'This is the first time we've seen either of you for twenty years. You said before that if it isn't what happened, it can't happen.'

'I…' The Doctor was lost for words. 'We must have… no. It's the plan, you see. A bit of Ghost of Christmas Future, just enough to make Alsa mend her ways – that was what that McDuck reference was all about. I really liked the McDuck reference.'

'You never came back. Is that bad?'

'It means…' the Doctor began, 'we must have got sidetracked. Or… worse.'

'You're so thick,' Alsa said.

'I'm not,' the Doctor objected. 'I'm great.'

'Don't you get it?'

The Doctor looked around, nonplussed.

'I get off here,' Alsa explained. 'I stay in the future. Can I come back, Dela? I know all about obstetrics.'

Dela raised an eyebrow.

'You don't have to,' the Doctor said. It wasn't clear if he meant that Alsa didn't have to stay or that Dela didn't have to take her. 'Although, come to think of it, that would work.'

'I just told you it would…' Alsa pointed out.

'I was talking in terms of the timeline,' the Doctor said airily.

'You can be a child here, Alsa,' Dela said. 'There are plenty of other children now. You can be grown up. Only if you want to, only when you're ready.'

The Doctor was beaming. 'There are choices here for you, now. Yes. The perfect solution. If anyone asks, this was the plan all along. What a great idea this was of mine.'

'You could stay, too, Doctor,' Dela said.

'Well,' he said, smile flashing, 'it wouldn't be fair on the rest of the universe, you having me all to yourself, would it?'

'Life's not fair,' Alsa noted.

The Doctor sniffed the air, turned on his heel, drank in the scene. He was lost in thought for a moment, then realised he'd placed his hand on the side of the TARDIS.

There was a big, wide universe out there and he had his second chance, too.

'Life's not fair?' he echoed. 'Well… I'll have to see what I can do about that.'

Acknowledgements

Thanks to Jon Blum, Graeme Burk, Mark Clapham, Mark Jones, Danielle Labbate, Philip Purser-Hallard, Kate Orman, Lars Pearson, Lloyd Rose, Jim Smith and Robert Smith. Thanks to the many and various behind the scenes people, including, but no doubt not limited to, Lee Binding, Albert DePetrillo, Caroline Newbury, Nicholas Payne, Gary Russell and Steve Tribe. Special thanks to Justin Richards and to Russell T Davies.

Also available from BBC Books featuring the Doctor and Donna as played by David Tennant and Catherine Tate:

Ghosts of India

by Mark Morris

ISBN 978 1 846 07559 9

UK £6.99 US $11.99/$14.99 CDN

India in 1947 is a country in the grip of chaos – a country torn apart by internal strife. When the Doctor and Donna arrive in Calcutta, they are instantly swept up in violent events.

Barely escaping with their lives, they discover that the city is rife with tales of 'half-made men', who roam the streets at night and steal people away. These creatures, it is said, are as white as salt and have only shadows where their eyes should be.

With help from India's great spiritual leader, Mohandas 'Mahatma' Gandhi, the Doctor and Donna set out to investigate these rumours.

What is the real truth behind the 'half-made men'? Why is Gandhi's role in history under threat? And has an ancient, all-powerful god of destruction really come back to wreak his vengeance upon the Earth?

Also available from BBC Books featuring the Doctor and Donna as played by David Tennant and Catherine Tate:

The Doctor Trap

by Simon Messingham

ISBN 978 1 846 07558 0
UK £6.99 US $11.99/$14.99 CDN

Sebastiene was perhaps once human. He might look like a nineteenth-century nobleman, but in truth he is a ruthless hunter. He likes nothing more than luring difficult opposition to a planet, then hunting them down for sport. And now he's caught them all – from Zargregs to Moogs, and even the odd Eternal...

In fact, Sebastiene is after only one more prize. For this trophy, he knows he is going to need help. He's brought together the finest hunters in the universe to play the most dangerous game for the deadliest quarry of them all.

They are hunting for the last of the Time Lords – the Doctor.

Also available from BBC Books featuring the Doctor and Donna as played by David Tennant and Catherine Tate:

Shining Darkness

by Mark Michalowski

ISBN 978 1 846 07557 5
UK £6.99 US $11.99/$14.99 CDN

For Donna Noble, the Andromeda galaxy is a long, long way from home. But even two and a half million light years from Earth, danger lurks around every corner…

A visit to an art gallery turns into a race across space to uncover the secret behind a shadowy organisation.

From the desert world of Karris to the interplanetary scrapyard of Junk, the Doctor and Donna discover that appearances can be deceptive, that enemies are lurking around every corner – and that the centuries-long peace between humans and machines may be about to come to an end.

Because waiting in the wings to bring chaos to the galaxy is the Cult of Shining Darkness.

Also available from BBC Books:

DOCTOR·WHO

The Time Traveller's Almanac

by Steve Tribe

ISBN 978 1 846 07572 8
£14.99

Who are the eminent artists of the 16th, 19th or 21st centuries? What are the mysteries of Carrionite science? Where do the Daleks come from? Answers to all of these questions and more are found in *The Time Traveller's Almanac*, the ultimate intergalactic fact-finder.

The *Almanac* draws on resources far and wide, from the beginning of time to the end of the universe, to provide information on key historical events and great lives, important issues in science, technology and the arts, and the stories that have defined each era.

Fully illustrated with photos and artwork, *The Time Traveller's Almanac* provides an essential biography of the *Doctor Who* universe.

Also available from BBC Books featuring the Doctor and Martha as played by David Tennant and Freema Agyeman:

The Story of Martha

by Dan Abnett

with David Roden, Steve Lockley & Paul Lewis, Robert Shearman, and Simon Jowett

ISBN 978 1 846 07561 2

UK £6.99 US $11.99/$14.99 CDN

For a year, while the Master ruled over Earth, Martha Jones travelled the world telling people stories about the Doctor. She told people of how the Doctor has saved them before, and how he will save them again.

This is that story. It tells of Martha's travels from her arrival on Earth as the Toclafane attacked and decimated the population through to her return to Britain to face the Master. It tells how she spread the word and told people about the Doctor. The story of how she survived that terrible year.

But it's more than that. This is also a collection of the stories she tells – the stories of adventures she had with the Doctor that we haven't heard about before. The stories that inspired and saved the world…

Also available from BBC Books featuring the Doctor and Donna as played by David Tennant and Catherine Tate:

Beautiful Chaos

by Gary Russell

ISBN 978 1 846 07563 6
UK £6.99 US $11.99/$14.99 CDN

Donna Noble is back home in London, catching up with her family and generally giving them all the gossip about her journeys. Her grandfather is especially overjoyed – he's discovered a new star and had it named after him. He takes the Doctor, as his special guest, to the naming ceremony.

But the Doctor is suspicious about some of the other changes he can see in Earth's heavens. Particularly that bright star, right there. No, not that one, that one, there, on the left…

The world's population is slowly being converted to a new path, a new way of thinking. Something is coming to Earth, an ancient force from the Dark Times. Something powerful, angry, and all-consuming…